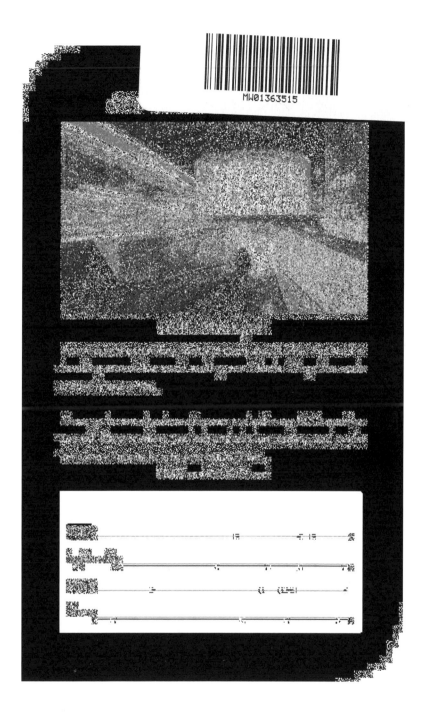

CONTROL THEORY

Copyright © Pedro Iniguez 2016
All Rights Reserved

The moral right of Pedro Iniguez to be identified as the author of this work has been asserted in accordance with the Copyright, Designs and Patents Act of 1988.
No part of this publication may be reproduced, stored in a retrieval system, or transmitted, in any form or by any means, electronic, mechanical, photocopying, recording, or otherwise, without the prior written permission of the publisher, nor be otherwise circulated in any form of binding or cover other than that in which it is published and without a similar condition being imposed on the subsequent purchaser.

All characters in this book are fictitious, and any resemblance to real persons, living, dead or not yet born, is coincidental.

A catalogue record for this book is available from the British Library.

ISBN: 978-1-910910-10-8

1st Edition

Indie Authors Press policy is to use paper that are natural, renewable, and recyclable products and made from wood grown in sustainable forests. The logging and manufacturing processes are expected to conform to the environmental regulations of the country of origin.

London | Chile | USA

ACKNOWLEDGMENTS

MANY THANKS TO RYAN Nelson, who so expertly edited this story and kept me in line. Also, to Chloe Camonayan who became my primary test reader and critic.

And finally, to all my friends and family, whose words of support were the fuel that kept the engine running on those long, long days.

~**Pedro Iniguez**~

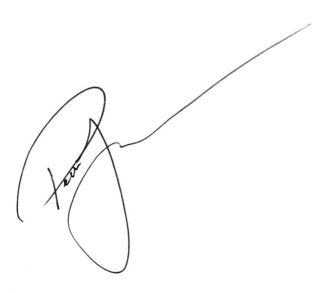

THIS BOOK IS FOR…

…Chloe,

who was the seed of inspiration for this story,

and whose love and dedication

kept me going.

To my mother, Maria,

whose quiet nurture and support

made all this possible.

PROLOGUE

THE RAIN FELL LIKE electric needles as the city lights bathed the water in their neon glow. A dome of smog and clouds encased the city as the aura of skyscrapers cast a grid of geometric shadows on the streets. Before he even stepped outside, Gerald Cromwell could hear the crackle of rain carpet-bombing the pavement. He stuffed his fingers into his leather gloves, bundled up in his raincoat, and stepped out into the cold Los Angeles air.

The rains hadn't come in over a year. The reservoir hadn't dragged in anything but piss and spit and Gerald thought the city could use the water. Maybe it would wash away some of the grime. And some of the people.

His driver, Sam, pulled up in his favorite set of wheels—an old, black Lincoln Town Car. Gerald's father had left him the car before his passing. His father told him Wall Street's elite used to own those cars when businessmen were still seen as symbols of honor. The good old days. Before the War. Before the Stock Market crash. Before the Red Crescent bombed Philadelphia.

Sam got out and ran to him holding an umbrella. "Sorry, Boss, had a hard time finding this thing. Hardly ever rains, you know?" Sam had a scar over his mouth where Gerald presumed he used to have a cleft lip. The misshapen fold that ran along his upper lip revolted him and he made a mental note to have Sam replaced soon.

"Just open the goddamn door."

Before he stepped in, Gerald turned around and looked up at Paradigm Tower, the mecca of bio-mechanical research. The spire loomed above the city like a monolith. A true wonder of the world. Gerald's gaze turned to the other towers. The buildings of the downtown skyline stood erect and tall like chrome dominoes. Entire portions of the sky were blotted out by their majesty depending on where one stood. What man could achieve when not burdened by regulations and bureaucracy was amazing. He took in a deep breath of the fresh, cold air, letting it fill his lungs. Rain smacked against his head. He wiped his face and stepped inside the car.

Gerald was met with warmth, and the pleasure of leather seats. He leaned his head back, closed his eyes, and sighed. *Fools. All of them.* They would be the downfall of Paradigm. The board was ready to collapse from its own lack of vision. Then again, that was nothing new. He shook his head. No. He wouldn't let that ruin his evening. Tonight, he would treat himself. He deserved it.

"I'm famished," Gerald said.

"Which fine restaurant tonight, Boss?" Sam asked as he started the engine.

"No restaurants."

Sam nodded and drove.

Gerald looked out the window. The crystalline facades of chrome over concrete faded in the distance as the Lincoln navigated the bumps of potholes and cracked asphalt. At the end of the workday, waves of men in fine, pressed suits crossed the street, slagging along like broken robots in need of a quick charge.

Orbs of neon wisped by his window, clashing for attention on every turn and corner. Advertisements flickered everywhere—arcades, food, strippers. Japanese letters blinked on and off outside the cybercafés, their dark and dingy hallways welcomed scores of depraved youth. Video Billboards looped at every red light, reminding drivers their petty lives wouldn't be complete without buying a new holoscreen or synth-pet for the family.

After a few minutes, the buildings, lights, suits, and ties disappeared completely. The attire of the city became hooded jackets, steel-toed boots, and shredded rags. Gerald grimaced. It never got easier being down among the filth. He could almost smell the stench of rainwater as it mixed with the vomit and piss-filled pavement of the back alleys.

The Lincoln weaved through the shifting scenery of the streets and boulevards. It always amused Gerald how Los Angeles wasn't a true metropolis but a patchwork of barrios, suburbs, and towns all festering in the shadows of the high-rises. Boutiques gave way to liquor stores. Vagrants lined the walls of abandoned cinemas as the warm lights of bustling café's flickered across the street. The silhouettes of palm trees swayed through broken slums as cell towers lined the sidewalks like sentries. There, amidst the paradox of Los Angeles, he saw the Blacks, the Hispanics, the Orientals clawing at each other's throats like the vermin they were. Stowaway rats, all of them.

He knew how to make the people go away.

He had been Chief Financial Officer at Paradigm Industries for over two decades. He hadn't gotten there without knowing how to play the game. His father had told him when he was a boy, *no one matters but you.* He'd turned his back on people that had once considered him a friend, but there were no regrets. As for the howls of the broken faces that haunted the streets, he could just drown out their voices. That was the name of the game. You just close your eyes and they all go away.

They arrived at Sunset Boulevard. The car pulled up to a dark stretch of curb, red heels lining the length of the embankment. The women clustered around his car like a flock of hungry seagulls, craning their necks at the sight of their next meal. They hollered and barked at their own reflections, trying desperately to sell their wares. Like small atomic bombs, the rain pelted their faces, causing a runoff of inky mascara to stream down their eyes. Lipstick-smeared teeth flashed and seemed to glow in the dark of the boulevard.

As he scanned their faces, he felt ill. Why had he stooped so low? He could have the best girl's money could buy. Had he gotten so bored that he had to resort to gutter meat? He frowned. None of them piqued his interest anyway.

"Sam, never mind. Start the car."

The engine rumbled and the women gave up the

charade, yelling obscenities and cursing his mother as they dispersed into the night. As they scattered, something caught Gerald's eye. The woman stood out from the trash around her. She looked striking just standing there in the rain as the water drenched her hair. She stared into his tinted window as if she could see him. She smiled.

She was tall. He liked that. He could already imagine those legs wrapping around his waist. She wore a short, leather skirt and a tight corset in red and black harlequin. Her hair was tidied up in double pigtails like a little girl on her first day of school.

"Sam, wait. Stop the car." The car broke a few feet from the curb. He rolled down the window. "You, in the harlequin dress. Come here, doll."

She hesitated, looked down at her feet, and then stepped forward. Ah, she was shy. A new girl. Well, he liked to break them in when they were still tight.

Harlequin approached the window with her head bowed down. She raised a hand to her mouth and chewed on her thumbnail like a nervous child. Gerald could see her blonde hair and blue eyes now. She didn't look filthy like the rest. She was young, no older than nineteen, he guessed. She reminded him of his step-daughter, Amelia. He smiled. "What's your name, sweetie?"

"Valerie."

"Valerie. What a pretty name. Valerie, do you want to come inside and keep me company? It's warm and dry in here. What do you say?"

She nodded. Gerald opened the door and shuffled aside. She slid inside and the car drove off. The Lincoln stopped at a red light, its warm glow illuminating her features. Her face was thickly powdered in white foundation as big, rosy blush circles painted her cheeks. She looked like a living doll. He had never been into role-play, but she was too gorgeous to pass up. He decided he'd take a little extra time with her. Besides, he told the wife he'd be out late at the office.

His fingers probed the inside of his coat. He retrieved a

small rectangular cartridge with a needle at the end of it. "You ever shoot Magma, Valerie?" he asked as he dangled the cartridge in front of her.

Valerie shook her head and crossed her legs like a polite little girl. She placed her hands on her lap and looked out the window.

Gerald took off his coat and rolled up his sleeve. A red light blinked on the top of the cartridge; it hissed as he injected the vein in his arm. He tossed it on the floor and leaned back. His eyes rolled back in his head. "It's a synthetic narcotic. Makes you feel like a million bucks. The box heats the juice up; you get a warm rush through your veins. Want some?"

She shook her head again.

"Too bad. People like you would kill for this."

She smiled— the only invitation he needed.

He placed his hand on her leg. His fingers crawled up her thigh like a tarantula. She didn't tremble. She was more experienced than he had thought. No matter— there was no stopping him now. His index and middle finger brushed her privates. She moaned, sounding cold and mechanical, free of any emotion.

Valerie unlaced her corset. Her breasts spilled out. They were small, like those of a young girl who hadn't reached sexual maturity.

The Magma raised his body temperature as beads of sweat trickled down his face. He loosened his tie and leaned in to kiss her neck. Her skin was still wet from the rain. He licked the water and felt a small relief from the heat.

Valerie leaned her head against the headrest and arched her back, pulling him in against her body. Gerald buried his face in her breasts.

His hand reached behind her head. He felt a small, cold protrusion. His hand slipped further down her spine and found jagged bumps. Metal. He looked up. Her blue eyes became blue lights, glowing in the dark of the Lincoln. Valerie wrapped her hands around his neck and squeezed.

Gerald gripped her wrist and pulled but couldn't break

her hold. Her small hands squeezed tighter. His fingernails buried into her skin and dug. Her skin ripped open, exposing thin metal cylinders sliding up and down as a clutter of cables weaved through them. His lungs burned as he gasped for air. The blood in his head felt like it was boiling now. His tongue wiggled up and down as he tried to simulate the sounds that would form the word "Sam."

Sam didn't hear.

One of the last things Gerald Cromwell heard was the sound of his own neck breaking. Like a branch snapping during a storm. The world started to fade. The voices of the filth that plagued his city started to fade away. That was the name of the game. You just close your eyes and they all go away.

***

CHAPTER ONE

LILY SANTOS DIDN'T BELIEVE in those sorts of things: trinkets, charms, whatever they were called. They had no true power. The only weight to them was sentimental, like an artefact given by a loved one. In this case her mother. But the small silver cross hung on her neck and kissed her cleavage all the same. She wasn't sure if wearing it was a smart choice; religious symbols tended to be frowned upon in the industry. She hoped it would be a fashion accessory and nothing more.

She checked her look in the mirror one more time. The black blouse with the plunging neckline was professional, but sexy. The skirt wasn't too short but flashed enough leg to set off a Pavlovian chain reaction. She used the right amount of eyeliner to accentuate her brown, almond-shaped eyes. That was key. Her features were considered exotic and it's what had gotten her noticed in the first place.

There weren't too many Filipino women around Los Angeles anymore, at least that she'd met, and the dark-skinned ones were considered unattractive by American standards. Her light skin was a gift; her mother had told her. She would've been happy being dark, but in this world, she had learned the benefits of a lighter complexion: it got you into more places that didn't involve jail or an early grave.

Her mother had always reminded her to know what she had and run with it. That was her mother, always resourceful. Rest her soul.

Before Lily turned away from the mirror she noticed something missing. Something to break the black monotony of her dress. She raised her hands. A gold watch perhaps. Lily's hand reached for the counter. Her fingers reached inside her jewelry box and prodded through cold brass and small gemstones. She felt the envelope and looked down. A letter from her bank. How long had it been there?

She tore open the envelope and read. As her eyes scanned the letter, she felt an odd pain; the pain of knowing all too well how alone she truly was in the world. She had felt the same emptiness in the pit of her stomach on two occasions. The first was on her first day of school in Los Angeles, alone in the company of countless giggling faces. The second she had felt when her mother passed.

Nocturne Magazine had rescinded payment for her last gig. She had walked out during a nude photoshoot. Even now the embarrassment swept over her as her cheeks flushed. She had stood in front of the spotlight, bare and exposed in front of strange faces, their eyes scrutinizing her every inch of flesh. She couldn't face the shame of it. A cold, hollow feeling had washed over her then. Was she just a body for strange men to ogle behind closed bathroom stalls? Just a pretty face to be exploited? Money was hard to come by, she knew that, but she remembered her mother's words. *Even in the certainty of darkness, you should always be your own light.*

Nocturne published the pictures and composited her face out of them. She couldn't prove it was her and so, there went the money. She had broken contract.

Lily looked at her calendar. Rent was due in five days.

She strapped on her mother's gold watch. She looked at it as it dangled just a little loosely on her wrist. She wondered if she would have to sell it before long.

Just like everything else.

Things in Los Angeles weren't ideal, but it was better than life in the Philippines. At least since the War. The Red Crescent— the collective might of North Korea, China, and Russia— had annexed her island home, stripping it from the soil-stained clutches of her people. What little national spirit lingered existed only in the old-timers who still held out hope for an American intervention that would never come.

How could she forget? She thought about the city of Ilagan. In the slums, deep down in the filth of the shantytowns, she remembered the daily pangs in her stomach while holding her mother's hands. The visions of men in red uniforms marching in the mush of the rice paddies still lingered vividly in her dreams. Her mother's words looped over and over in her head. Never let go. Never leave my sight. Or had Lily said that?

Her mother traded the pangs of Ilagan for the pangs of Los Angeles on a stowaway ticket for two. Somehow, the fishing vessel hadn't been blown away by Red Crescent gunships. For that she was grateful. Despite the potential harm that might have befallen them on their journey, the risk had been worth it. In Llagan you never knew what the day would bring: a warm meal; the coin of a generous tourist; a night's sleep in the damp night air as the rockets lit the sky like fireworks. In Los Angeles, they had still lived among the filth, but it was a stable kind of squalor. She found it humorous. Stable squalor: the American Dream.

She walked to the window. It had stopped raining for now. Dirty runoff trickled down the awnings, culminating in grey waterfalls as they cascaded onto the sidewalks below. In the distance, neon lights glistened all the way to the razor's edge of the horizon. The firefly lights of cars on the freeway twinkled in a slow, never-ending procession. A few random police drones buzzed the sky like black-matted vultures, their red-and-blue lights twinkling like stars. The city was a labyrinth of streets and lights. Sometimes she wondered if there was a way out.

Lily looked down. A buzzing lamppost flickered violently and gave out like an animal in its death throes. Fitting. She couldn't think of a better analogy for her neighborhood. A dying animal.

It had been a struggle. She had no formal education besides the theatre classes she had taken at night, and her accent couldn't even get her a simple secretarial job. The income from the occasional modelling gig or small clothing line amounted to nothing more than scraps and crumbs.

But tonight was her big break. Tonight would be

different.

She walked to the answering machine and played the message again, just to make sure it was real. Her agent, Cody DelMonde, came alive in the form of a fragmented hologram recording. His image sizzled and shifted through the small projector of her cheap vidbox. Motes of dust mingled with a spray of spit as he cleared his throat.

"Lily, honey, I've got some great news. But it's urgent. I got you an audition. Hell, it's almost a guarantee. It's this movie 'Tempest in Tokyo'. The lead, Monica Yoshida, has been a no-show for a couple days now and they need a beautiful Asian actress who can speak English. That's it. Minimal dialogue, too. But, listen, it's at seven tonight. Check your email, I've already sent you the address. I'm gonna let them know you're coming. This is what we've been waiting for, Lily. And if you get it I'm only helping myself to a measly twenty percent. That's it. Keep me updated."

He vanished into the vidbox like a ghost.

Never hesitate to pick up somebody else's pieces, she'd heard once. She wasn't going to pass up an opportunity like this. The audition was unusually late in the evening and her legs ached from all the walking she had done as she went business to business looking for gigs, but that wasn't going to stop her.

She stepped toward her front door. The anxiety kicked in like a jolt through her nervous system as the hairs on her neck went prickly. She had never done something this big. Would she forget her lines? Would she be pretty enough? Would her accent be too off-putting? Her body froze and the world around her came to life: the sound of cars motoring by, honking like some schizophrenic jazz number; the drunken footfalls of hustlers as their shoes tapped on the streets like distant knocks; advertisements shouting lies to their homeless audiences on the sidewalks.

And the Holoscreen, almost as if feeding off her fears, had a story tailor-made for her. The anchor straightened up and pulled on his tie, adding to the gravity of the situation as he looked straight into the camera. "Ladies and gentlemen, the string of missing women, the highest reported in September, continues tonight, as Japanese-American actress Monica Yoshida, is now believed to have gone missing."

Lily didn't know why, she didn't believe in those sorts of things, but she gripped the cross at her chest, whispered a prayer, and walked out the door.

***

CHAPTER TWO

DETECTIVE AUDRIC DEVEREUX PLACED a hand on his chest and took a deep breath. The pacemaker was still holding up. He told himself the tightness in his chest was just the cold air. He exhaled and wisps of vapor escaped his lips.

The sirens wailed as the LED's flashed red and blue; their lights spitting webs of gnarled shadows across the wet streets. He spotted the camera crews hovering over the scene like flies. In a tangle of elbows, batons, and cameras, uniformed officers held the reporters back like warriors on an ancient battlefield. A member of the press— a young man in a fedora with a lumberjack beard- made eye contact with him and took a step forward. He looked like one of those armchair internet video reporters cops despised. Devereux spat on the floor and the reporter retreated to his spot.

Devereux smirked and ducked under the yellow tape.

Sunset Boulevard. An old black Lincoln sat idly crooked in the middle of the street. The rear right door hung open. Under it, a large man lay on the asphalt, splayed out like a big, white starfish. Detective Michael Kinneman stood watch over a corpse dressed in a white button-up shirt and burgundy tie. The shirt had soaked up the water from the damp street partially revealing the man's skin underneath.

"Hello, Detective Kinneman. Sorry I'm late. I was hoping to beat the reporters this time."

"You know that's not possible," Kinneman said smiling. He was tall, blonde and what people liked to call statuesque. "Pretty soon these guys are gonna have our jobs. Good to see you, Detective Devereux." Kinneman shook Devereux's hand and nodded at the body. Devereux squatted and reached inside his raincoat for latex gloves. He knelt beside the corpse and gently moved the man's chin left, then right. Long, red streaks marked his doughy neck. A hand-print. The victim, an overweight Caucasian male, late fifties perhaps, stared blankly at the night sky.

"Who is he?"

Kinneman glossed over his PDA. "His identification lists him as Gerald Cromwell, fifty-eight. CFO of Paradigm Industries. No criminal record. Lived in a condo way up there," he said pointing to the skyscrapers lurching over the downtown skyline.

"So, he was rich. Anything else?"

"Yeah, his driver didn't fare well either. Right this way."

Kinneman led Devereux to the driver's side door where it also stood open. Kinneman tilted his head. Blood, like red molasses, seeped down the door, dripping onto the street, mixing with the oil and rainwater, creating a psychedelic puddle. Devereux peered in. A black man sat at the helm of the car, his eyes fixed on something past the windshield. The flesh from his cheeks had stretched and torn, leaving gaps of exposed sinew and bone. His lower jaw hung eight inches below where it should have as thin strands of skin were all that kept if from falling off. He touched the man's jowls with a gloved hand. The blood was sticky. It had poured down the man's neck, chest, and torso and dried inside the warm car.

"His I.D. lists him as Samuel Beaudry Levine," Kinneman said. "A licensed driver for the high class. He lives...lived, I should say, in Boyle Heights, so I'm assuming he was poorer than dirt."

"His jaw was completely unhinged," Devereux said turning to Detective Kinneman. "What kind of force could do that?"

He sighed. "We don't know, but look there," Kinneman said, shining his flashlight behind Levine. The light caught the serrated edge of the broken window that separated driver and passenger. "Looks like whoever killed Cromwell smashed the glass here and reached inside," he said shining the light at Levine, "and did this. No traces of blood on the glass, either." He looked back at Devereux.

"This door. Levine opened it?"

"Looks like the driver opened the door to flee. Unsuccessfully." Kinneman shook his head in feigned disgust he had no doubt practiced over and over. He retrieved a pack of cheap cigarettes from his coat. He lit up and extended his hand, offering Devereux the pack. Devereux waved it off. "We don't know much, but we do know that it appears Mr. Cromwell was asphyxiated. Maybe even a broken neck. As to which killed him first? I don't know. I'm guessing the broken neck." Kinneman exhaled, the smoke mingling with the vapor as it left his mouth.

Devereux turned away from the smoke. "Robbery?"

"It doesn't appear as if anything was stolen from his person. We checked his leather. Couple hundred-dollar bills and some credit cards still in there."

"Do we have any drone surveillance video?"

"No drones were buzzing this area when the crime occurred."

The police department utilized a handful of autonomous surveillance drones. They flew above the L.A. skies at all times of the day, but Devereux had known their flight paths were based on randomly generated algorithms based on crime statistics.

"Mm. Brutal case you boys in Homicide have on your hands. Why call me?"

"We questioned one of the girls that works the streets here."

"A call girl?"

"They all scattered when we showed up, but we did manage to snatch one up for questioning. Goes by the name of Melina. Says she saw a tall, skinny, dolled up girl get in the car before it drove off. Melina didn't recognize her; she apparently doesn't run in her clique. The pimps won't speak to us, mostly because as soon as they saw us, they turned tail. We also found an empty cartridge of Magma on the car floor, next to where we believe Mr. Cromwell was sitting. This looks like a Vice job too, Devereux. You're being assigned to parallel and assist this investigation. Sorry."

Devereux looked at Kinneman with a glassy stare, then shifted his eyes to his watch. Friday, September 26th. The time was 6:30. His shift was half an hour away from being over. It had been a long day slogging through files and writing reports as he put the finishing touches on his last case. Crime never slept. Why should he? He cursed under his breath and turned to Sam. His tongue hung limp in that wide gape of astonishment he died in. Or was it fear? Devereux had been on the force a long time; enough to know this one was strange. Sure, sex, drugs, and murder were older than sin itself, but this was different. A young call girl crushing a man's windpipe, one who likely had a sizeable weight advantage? Sure, plausible. Likely? No. Same call girl getting the jump on the driver and unhinging his entire lower jaw? Impossible.

He wasn't a homicide detective but he could help by starting to question some of the bottom-feeders who might have some answers.

He turned to the man formerly known as Samuel Beaudry Levine. He was well dressed for a driver. Blazer, vest, nice grey slacks. Devereux wondered if the uniform came with the job, or if he had to pay for it out of pocket. Probably the latter, the poor sap. Devereux lifted Levine's blazer aside and reached into his vest pocket. A matchbook. In fiery red and orange text the words *Hades* scorched boldly across. Familiar name. He'd heard it before but no details came to mind. He made a note to look into it. Devereux stuffed the matches in his coat and stepped away.

He turned to face the skyscrapers. Mr. Cromwell lived up there with the angels but came down here to slap skins with the devils. No one was innocent in this town. Even in the city of angels, every saint had his vice.

Devereux ducked under the tape and turned away from the scene. He stuffed his hands in his coat pockets and started to walk across the dark, wet street. Melina was standing there, leaning against a filthy wall, glaring at the scene in front of her. So many men and not a single one was buying. He turned to Kinneman, the embers of his cigarette flickering as he took one last drag. "I'll look into it."

SHE SMELLED LIKE MARIJUANA and sex so Devereux knew it was a good place to start. Her name was Melina Fina and she had lingered a little too long waiting for her pimp to arrive. She had no choice. It was their designated pickup spot, and it just so happened that a double homicide occurred there. She had already been through questioning, but he figured he'd take a crack at it.

Melina was a short, cute Latina girl, twenty-five years old. She wore a white crop top, revealing her bare midriff, as she sported a short, red skirt. Classic hooker uniform. She had more curves than a sidewinder, and was probably just as venomous.

"I told them already, I didn't see anything," she said gritting her teeth behind her full, red lips.

"Well, I'm not them," Devereux said. "Tell me what you did see."

She clenched her fists. Fire in her veins. Or was it poison? "Like I said already, this car pulls up to me and my friends and this fat guy starts eyeing us all creeper-like, so we walk away. I turned around again and someone else is getting in."

"Did you see who got in?"

"I mostly saw her back. She was tall, maybe like five-eleven. Pale legs, and blonde hair, so I'm guessing white girl? I didn't even notice her. She kind of just came out of nowhere. The other girls saw her. Said she had a lot of makeup on."

Devereux nodded as he scribbled in his notebook. "Anything unique about her makeup? Anything easily identifiable? Scars?"

He looked up. She bit her lips and rolled her eyes in what he assumed was anger or impatience. Her hand hovered around her waist. Cornered hookers had been known to stick cops and make a break-for-it. As he scanned her waist, he caught sight of a scar, like a lightning bolt across her belly.

"One of the girls said she had big red blush marks on her cheeks. Super caked on. Said her face was white as a ghost."

He nodded again.

"What happened then? The driver's dead. Why didn't the

car crash into a lamppost or something?"

"The hell should I know? The car stopped at a red light, drove for a few more seconds, and then broke hard in the middle of the street. I saw the girl step out and run into that alley," she said pointing north.

About twenty yards ahead, a small alley divided the block. Devereux nodded. "Thanks Melina, you've been very helpful. Here," he said as he reached into his pocket. Devereux pulled out a fifty-dollar bill and extended his hand. "Buy your kid some dinner."

"How did-"

"The caesarean scar on your belly. Don't let me catch you doing anything illegal next time I'm out here." She took the bill with shaky hand. She opened her mouth.

He didn't wait around to hear what she had to say.

He walked ahead toward the tail end of Sunset Boulevard, away from the raucous bars, strip joints, and general noise pollution that was rooted in the DNA of Hollywood. Nothing but liquor stores, donut shops, and girls. And boys, depending where you looked.

He turned right. The brick alley was narrow and uneven as it cut through two rows of back doors and fire exits. An overflowing dumpster sat crooked and dented against the wall, probably forgotten by sanitation worker's years ago. Above, the sound of broken heaters sputtered by shattered apartment windows.

A soft scratch came from behind the trash heap. He put a hand on his holster and stepped forward. He peeked behind the dumpster. An old man sat against the brick wall, mumbling to himself in the darkness. A gust of wind howled through the alley, giving life to the scent of urine and body odor.

"Hi," Devereux said as he flashed his badge and a half-smile. His right hand hovered above the holster. Kinneman hadn't mentioned questioning any vagrants in his initial briefing. "Detective Devereux. Mind if I ask you some questions?"

The man tilted his head upwards, scanned Devereux, and then looked back down. "Fuck off."

Devereux knelt beside him. "You know what I can do, right? You know I'm within my legal right to turn you over to the war effort? I hope you like China because I hear they've taken to eating people nowadays. Or maybe you'll get lucky and take a neural flechette in the eye, let the nanobots eat your brain instead. All I have to do is call an Urban Recruiter and he'll ship you off tonight."

The old man looked up at the wall as if to ponder the statement and then smirked, shifting his grey beard. "Can't do a damn thing. They only take the young ones. The strong ones."

Devereux frowned. "Knowledge is power. But so is this," he said as he retrieved a five-dollar bill from his pocket. "Might be enough to get you a warm coffee if you find the right spot."

The old man reached out his hand.

"Talk first. Your name?"

The old man rubbed his chin and furrowed his brows as if searching the depths of his memory bank. "Willie Parker. Hard to remember when no one talks to you."

"Hello, Willie. Were you here a little while ago, before the police showed up?"

Willie nodded his head.

"We could've used some witnesses back there."

"I don't like the police. They're bullies with guns," he said flashing a toothless smile.

"I'm different, Willie" Devereux said smiling. "Think of me as a social worker with a gun." He'd used the same line before on vagrants. They hardly ever bought it.

Willie looked at the wrinkled fiver in front of him. Another gust blew in. The homeless man pulled his coat tight against his chest. "Ask."

"The black car down the street. Two dead. What did you see?"

Willie grumbled something under his breath. "Won't matter. I was tripping."

"Like stumbling?"

"No, like *drogas*."

"Try me."

"I was coming off a daze," he said. "This villainous Mexican weed I scored the other day had me down and out. The screech woke me. Sounded like an angry Thunderbird. The car broke in the middle of the street. And I mean broke hard, boy. Then I saw the damnedest thing. This girl gets out the car and drags this big guy's body and dumps him out onto the street. Only thing was her eyes, they were glowing blue. Fucking blue."

"You think it might've been a headlamp?"

"No, her *eyes*," he shouted, exasperated, pointing to his own pair.

Devereux stopped scribbling. "What then?"

"She ran through the alley and that's that. Totally ignored me, so that's good."

"Mm. Tell me something. Was she stumbling, or running off-center?"

"Hell no. She was running like a track star," he said rubbing his index and middle finger back and forth, mimicking the act of running. "Straight and true."

Willie's statement eliminated a few avenues. If she was on something it wasn't Magma, which didn't appear to be stolen. Magma dulled the senses, nearly put users out for the count. The stuff was basically heroin in new duds. Whoever invented it dressed it up in a fancy electric cartridge and marketed it to a strictly affluent market.

It didn't mean she wasn't on something, it just meant it wasn't a downer. That left the extreme feats of strength: He'd once witnessed a PCP user who punched straight through an Interceptor windshield without feeling the slightest bit of pain. The drug induced feelings of power and invincibility. It was a possibility but there wasn't much to go on there. PCP was manufactured everywhere: dirty basement labs, across the border. Pinpointing a distributor would be difficult. Magma on the other hand he could narrow down. Maybe he could get a bead on who sold it to Cromwell and take it from there.

He handed Willie the bill. Willie smiled and saluted him.

"This is off the record, old-timer, but," Devereux said as he reached inside his coat. He retrieved a faded wallet-sized photo and handed it to Willie. "Have you seen this man? Picture's from at least fifteen years ago."

He handed Willie a portrait of a young man who could have just escaped the purgatory stages of growing pains and puberty. His dark hair swept across one eye like an eyepatch while the other half of his head was shaved clean; either in rebellion or in attempt to define himself as different like most boys that age. Some sort of wisdom lived inside his weary brown eyes, deep, beyond the heavy bags underneath them. Missing on the photograph was a time stamp and a smile.

Willie squinted in the dark of the alley. "He someone important?"

"Something like that."

"He's gone."

"You know him?"

"Don't need to. Sooner or later we're all gone. He just got it sooner," Willie said as he handed the picture back, laughing.

Devereux turned and left the dark of the alley. He put his hands in his coat pockets, and like a moth, he headed toward the lights of the city.

***

CHAPTER THREE

THE RAINS HAD STOPPED for the most part, but grey clouds still lingered reluctantly over the sky like great Chinese dragons. It was just a lull in the storm. The aura of blue street lights illuminated the small beads of moisture still falling from the sky as the neon puddles rippled with every drop, like a moving watercolor painting.

Lily approached the crosswalk and waited for the light to change. She looked left and then right. Nothing but cracked asphalt and a street empty of cars. Besides the distant murmur of the city, it was unusually quiet. This time usually belonged to the pepped-out hoodlums and silver-tongued con-men. She'd been taught to always be aware of her surroundings. Her mother had even made her take a few Eskrima classes when she was a girl. Knowledge instilled in her since before she moved to Los Angeles when she was fifteen. She almost couldn't believe it. Had it already been twelve years?

As she looked around her, there were flashes of Ilagan everywhere; in a way, it had prepared her for living in Los Angeles. Even here, the transients set up their village of tents and trash bag forts. And like home, the sidewalks were lined with rusty shopping carts and huddled piles of clothing she assumed people were sleeping under.

Lily looked behind her. Nothing but the crumbling structure she called home. The building looked like it was a 3.2 magnitude earthquake away from collapsing to dust. And all it cost her was most of her paycheck. Cody had told her all the stars started out that way. *Humble beginnings, baby.*

She frowned the more she thought about it. Had she had

friends, she might have found herself embarrassed to live there. But that was the case most everywhere, she assumed. Her city was an amalgamation of socio-economic conditions. The decaying buildings and apartments housed struggling musicians, eccentric beatniks, and down-and-out textile workers. The streets belonged to the vagabonds and the homeless or the strung-out junkies and squatters who crawled into black holes to fade away and die. The condos and the high-rises belonged to the wealthy and powerful who smiled as they watched the bottom feeders succumb to the slow decay of poverty.

That was Los Angeles though: it was the trickle-down city. A metropolis with its own multi-level ecosystem. When high society had given up on the people on the streets, they just built higher and higher, until the people down there were just drops of water in an ocean at night.

The light turned green and she hurried across, her heels clicking on the pavement. The taps echoed down the length of the empty street. She pulled her blazer in tight to stave off the cold. As she reached the bus stop on the corner, a video billboard with a cracked screen looped a clip of a square-jawed man smiling, over and over again. A two-year-old commercial stalled for all eternity. Even the marketing departments had abandoned the people, leaving behind only the memory of a lustrous smile.

She glanced at her watch: 6:35 PM. Any minute now. Lily chose the driest spot she could find and sat on the bench next to the billboard. She looked around again. Her only company was laid out on the floor: a newspaper's picture of a Korean dictator rambling on about the War. She started to read the headline when a gust of wind blew in and carried her tyrannical friend away.

A flickering fluorescent bulb above the bench illuminated the tiny shadows at Lily's feet. The mice scurried on a trail along the floor and up an overflowing trash can, gnawing away at candy wrappers and empty pizza boxes. The vermin always came to claim their riches in the shadows. Lily stood and stepped aside. She looked down the street. Nothing.

A gust of cold air nipped at her legs and she tried in vain to pull her short skirt down her legs. She shivered and thought about the homeless who called the streets home and shrugged it off.

She hoped she hadn't missed her bus. The next one wasn't due for another hour and by then it would be too late.

No, don't think about it. Everything will be okay, you'll see.

She popped in her earphones, closed her eyes, and let the soothing trance of her music take hold.

A pair of headlights cut through the dark. Lily opened her eyes. An off-white van with a dented passenger door pulled up beside her. Her music had masked its approach. A man in a black parka hopped out and left the engine running.

He walked toward her, his face shrouded by the hood on his head. She took a step back. His lips moved but she didn't understand. She shook her head. He pointed to his wrist and looked at Lily inquisitively. *The time?*

She looked at her watch. A hand reached for her mouth and another swung around and wrapped around her torso. Her earphones popped out. She heard the faint sound of music and her own gasps as cold fingers squeezed her jaw. Lily tried to scream but the man clamped her mouth shut. She took a step back and her foot landed in a cold puddle. The water splashed, sending mice scattering.

An icy sting pierced her neck. Lily felt her legs go limp. Her eyes grew heavy and her world went as dark as the night.

The man hauled off his cargo and the van pulled away. The streets went quiet and they belonged once again to the scurry of mice.

***

CHAPTER FOUR

THE MANAGER AT THE cyber café shuffled nervously across the floor to intercept Devereux as he shoved through waves of kids in VR mounted headgear. The VR headsets looked like a combination of sunglasses and a botched attempt at a cathode ray tube. Wires wound and weaved their way around their heads and arms like living marionettes. Puppets to the program—slaves to code.

As he walked down the hall, Devereux caught a whiff of marijuana, cigarettes and things he wasn't sure of as they stood staring into invisible utopias. They grasped at items unseen and smiled through black gums and crooked teeth. Their muscles had begun to atrophy as their brains rotted inside the shells they called their bodies. The youngest appeared to be twelve years old and no more than a skeleton in an extra-large t-shirt. His bony arms cocked an invisible shotgun probably too heavy even in make-believe world. Devereux shook his head and wondered where their parents where.

He found an empty terminal by an empty corner of the room and swiped his Access Card across the strip reader. A green light blinked. The computer accepted his card, prompting a cold, synthetic greeting in an androgynous voice. "Hello, Detective Devereux. This is LAPDOG. How may I assist you this fine evening?"

"Computer, is this server secure?"

"Los Angeles Police Department Online Guide has overridden local software. Secure and ready for instruction."

A blank, green screen appeared on the monitor. A white, oblong bubble appeared at its center that read *Nexus*. The Nexus was the LAPD's center of inquiry; all avenues branched out from the Nexus allowing the user to return to the start and retrace all steps without getting too confused during an investigation. The program was essentially an interactive bubble diagram for stupid cops. Devereux had no problem with it. Not for his sake but for theirs.

The manager caught up to him, panting. The power walk down the café had been more work than he had probably done in years. Sweat dripped down his pockmarked face. He was just a kid, too, no older than eighteen years old.

"Sir, I'm afraid you'll have to log in and provide us with a credit card. This is not a library."

"Detective Devereux. Official police business. I'm commandeering a terminal. The city will reimburse you for all data usage."

The kid stood in place, confused. "Oh... so, that's it?"

"That's it," said Devereux. "Have a good one."

The kid shrugged, walked back to his desk, and kicked up his feet. He picked up a headset and plugged in.

"Computer, check messages."

A white line shot out from the Nexus, forming a smaller white bubble to the left that read *Messages*. He touched the monitor and selected it. One unread message awaited him as it blinked red. An alert from Kinneman.

Dev:

Questioned Cromwell's wife. No debts, no known enemies. Awaiting forensics to see if any other DNA matches found inside car. Autopsy report pending. Levine had no immediate family. No debt besides the standard credit card variety. Questioned neighbors: no known enemies. Autopsy report pending. Keep you updated. You do same.

Kinn

Devereux tapped the center of the screen. The Nexus bubble popped up again.

"Computer, what chemical component is found in Magma?"

A small bubble appeared above Nexus. "Diamorphine,"

the computer spoke. "Grade four Diamorphine, also known simply as Morphine. Grade four is easily dissolvable for interveinal use. The drug is used in hospitals to treat severe pain or on occasion, as an illicit recreational relaxant."

"Computer, look up local manufacturers of Diamorphine. Fifty-mile radius."

Another white bubble appeared on the screen above his previous inquiry. *Manufacturers*. The bubble split into four sub-bubbles to the right.

Devereux rubbed his chin. Four manufacturers within spitting distance. Names he couldn't even pronounce.

"Computer, have any of these companies been cited for ethical misconduct or grievances?"

A small bubble, *Grievances*, now sprang above the last bubble, forming a chain that reminded Devereux of one of those genome sequences or chemical composition pictures.

"Zylvan Corporation, Orange County pharmaceutical company, has a grievance currently under file and is pending investigation at the Los Angeles Business Bureau's office," the computer said.

"Elaborate," said Devereux as he pulled in a chair and sat.

"Filed August fifteenth by Bloom Memorial Hospital. Numerous accounts of incomplete shipments of Diamorphine received. Referencing police records… Zylvan Corporation has filed two reports of theft on large shipments while in transit."

He'd seen it done before. One of his earliest cases in Vice entailed similar characteristics. They must have been covering their own ass. Shrewd. And crooked. It looked like Zylvan was shipping off their merchandise only to have some of it mysteriously go missing. By reporting it as stolen, they were washing their hands of any wrongdoing. Since it could take months for the police to investigate— if ever— Zylvan could buy itself some time to cook up some healthy illicit business.

"Who runs this company? Look into grievances and criminal records," he said.

A bubble with the name *Vincent Karpanian* popped up. "Karpanian, Vincent, CEO. No criminal record. Majority owner of

Hades nightclub, located on Temple and Main Street."

Devereux straightened in his chair. He reached in his coat pocket and retrieved the matchbook. *Hades*. That's where he'd heard the name before. The infamous nightclub that catered to the city's elite. No one could get in without the proper financial credentials. Someone of Cromwell's status wouldn't have a hard time getting past the bouncer.

"Computer, look into Hades. Criminal occurrences and citations."

The inquiry formed a bubble around the word *Hades*. The computer spoke: "Aquino, Miguel, part-owner, was arrested for possessing banned stimulants. Various women cited for prostitution have also stated on the record that Hades manages an illicit prostitution ring on its premises. Statements not substantiated."

Devereux sighed. "Nexus," he said. The bubbles flew backwards as the cursor traced back the white lines like a spider on a web. *Hades*; *Karpanian*; *Grievances*; *Manufacturers*; *Diamorphine*.

Karpanian had access to wealthy clients and pharmaceuticals— specifically morphine— which happened to be missing lately. Great business model. Stealing your own merchandise and selling it to your rich patrons. Not much to pin on Zylvan unless the stolen merchandise could be traced to them. No way in hell Karpanian would subject himself to questioning. He'd surround himself with lawyers at the first sign of trouble.

He turned around. The kids swung their limbs awkwardly like puppets on strings. They were pantomiming as their make-believe world flashed before their eyes and the real one passed them by.

Make-believe.

He reached in his pocket and snatched his phone. He punched in some numbers and waited on the tone. On the other end, forensic investigator Walter Seamus answered.

"Hello?" asked Seamus.

Devereux paused. He wasn't typically one to ask.

Screw it.
"I need a big favor."

***

CHAPTER FIVE

LILY OPENED HER EYES and felt like throwing up. She saw only darkness. A draft blew in. She brought her arms against her chest and she knew then she was naked. She had woken from a nightmare. There had been a raspy voice in her head, like a rake scraping against gravel. The voice told her everything was going to be alright. It had all felt so real. Even the sharp sting to her spine had made her thrash. But the worst part of the dream had been the drone of power tools, grinding into something wet.

She turned her head to the right. Her vision spun. After a moment, the faint shape of objects started to form around her. A sharp, piercing pain throbbed deep behind her eyes as they tried to adjust to the darkness. The shapes looked strange, alien. The nausea crept in again. She let herself be still. She took deep breaths, letting the cold air fill her chest. She fought the urge to vomit as she felt a tug in her guts. A computer monitor lit the darkness, washing part of the room in a faint red light. Her eyes started to adjust. She could see the orange crust of oxidation taking hold on the steel wall next to it. Wires snaked their way through a blinking computer tower and ran through small holes in the floor where a rat scurried along mazes of rotting books. She wondered if she was still dreaming.

Water dripped sporadically and echoed in some unseen corner of the room. The resonance of the echoes told her the room was spacious.

A small aluminum table beside her came into focus. Green cloth lined the top tray, exposing a variety of sharp, shiny blades and serrated saws. The instruments were dripping red fluid, forming blotches on the cloth. She felt her heart thump against her chest.

She opened her mouth to say "Hello", but it was dry and no words formed. She wanted a drink of water. She licked her parched, cracked lips and tasted copper. She swallowed what little saliva she had and felt tightness in her throat.

The sound of furious clicking caught her attention. She turned to her left.

Click. Click. Click. Whirrrrr.

A man sat at a sewing machine in the shadows. A green surgical face mask concealed most of his face. A headlamp sat atop his head, shining a bright blue beam of light while his hands weaved side to side, guiding fabric across the pounding needle. What was he making? She squinted and it came into focus: a small black leather corset.

The man pedaled his feet, guiding the leather delicately. He worked like a man in a trance, his vision too narrow to notice anything else.

Lily tried to sit up slowly. Her arms felt heavy as she pushed against the table. Her fingers felt numb as they probed for texture. A sense of static coursed through her veins culminating on her fingertips. Her touch wasn't her own. She sat up. A sudden soreness pulsed at the back of her head now. With her index and middle finger, she prodded the back of her skull and felt a ring of cold metal. The surface was round and flat and no bigger than two inches across. She ran her hand further down her neck. Small, hard protrusions lined her dermis like the spine of a reptile. Like a punch in the stomach, Lily felt all the oxygen in her lungs sucked out of her. The thump of her heart raced faster.

She quickly swung her legs over the counter. On the far end of the room, something caught her eye. She was a young blonde woman and she couldn't have been older than a college freshman. She was naked and slumped on her side, staring back silently as the glow of red light outlined her pale skin. A layer of cracked, white makeup painted the woman's face like a mime.

Lily waved her hand in a small side-to-side motion. "Hey," she whispered. "Hey." The woman said nothing. Lily watched the woman's eyes. The dead blue orbs didn't shift or cry or blink. They just stared at the black floor.

Lily leaned her head over the table and regurgitated. The bitter taste of bile was revolting on her tongue. She looked away from the corpse and noticed another woman propped naked against the opposite corner. The woman looked familiar, the face ingrained somewhere in Lily's memory bank. The woman was Asian, young. Dried blood stained her blue lips and her arms were folded around her chest. The back of her head looked like it had been shaved in a hurry as portions of hair were thicker in some areas than others. The woman had beautiful, familiar eyes. Then it came and it hit Lily hard. Monica Yoshida. Actress in all those high-tech ninja movies they screened late at night. Monica Yoshida. Dead.

Lily stood. Her legs wobbled. She rested a hand against the tray. She pushed off and the tray flipped, spilling its sharp contents on the floor. The tiny pings of metal echoed through the room.

Just then the tailor in the shadows turned to her; his headlamp blinded her. "Now, now, my lovely, little doll. Let's not scream and wake the other girls."

He stood and shut off the headlamp. His body faded into the darkness of the room. She heard his footfalls near. Her hands brushed the rusted wall as she looked for a door. Nothing. She banged a knee against something solid. Her legs buckled at the pain and she stumbled to the floor.

The man stood above her. He reached for her face.

Lily opened her mouth. Not a sound escaped. In the dark of the room, Lily found her screams were as much a prisoner as she was.

***

CHAPTER SIX

BY THE TIME DEVEREUX got there a line of misfits had snaked around the block twice over. Temple and Main Street: the epicenter of weekend debauchery. The long downtown streets stretched for miles and hosted the hippest bars, clubs, massage parlors, and every other sensory festival known to man. The area was a hotbed for *drogas*, drinking, and death. Muggers, rich kids, RATS, and every kind of street punk and degenerate intermingled here as they quested for the next big thrill.

The kids outside this joint were of a particular ilk. Mostly they were wealthy young men and women looking to get drunk and score a hot date to bring home, all under the pretense of dancing to undanceable music. There were a few old-timers saucing it up with some of the girls as they dabbed in nose candy from the backs of their hands. The boys looked like clones with their slicked-back hair, damped in scented oils probably imported from the wastelands of Morocco or some other foreign hellhole. They strutted in colorful shirts, unbuttoned all the way down to their sternum, and black, silken slacks with perfectly pressed creases shooting down to their ankles. The girls wore short skirts and assless chaps and what were referred to as mop tops: form fitting blouses tasseled in thin strips of fabric hanging down their breasts.

An old Mexican woman wrapped in a thick, brown shawl, walked up and down the line pushing a shopping cart full of bouquets. She plucked a rose and held it up in the air like an offering to an unseen god. "*Rosas! Rosas!*" she said. Some of the men waved her over and swiped their cards on her portable terminal. The pretty girls plunged their noses into the petals and inhaled, smiling as the sweet fragrance of Delirium settled in their lungs.

Devereux walked up to the woman and said, "*Policía.*" She raised an eyebrow. He flipped his badge and she flipped the cart. She broke for the side streets as the crowd watched in indifference. Devereux plucked a rose from the floor and looked inside the petals. Blue dust: the synthesized extract of deadly nightshade. Delirium, they called it, an anticholinergic drug that caused cognitive disruption and gave its users the feeling of sleepwalking. He stepped over the flowers, their petals crushing under his heels.

He walked under an arched door, the word *Hades* blinked repeatedly in fiery electric text. The sonic assault barraged Devereux's ears from even outside: the thumping of the heavy drums, the vibrating bass, and the piercing synth notes. He took a deep breath as he felt the vibrations rumble in his chest.

The bouncer was a bald man, tall and built. He could've played football or been a bruiser in the Army. An electric prosthetic covered the socket where Devereux assumed he had lost an eye. Essentially, it was a monocle that transmitted images and processed them inside the brain— expensive augmentation. The bouncer must have had a very nice friend behind those doors. Devereux approached and the eyepiece dilated and then shrunk as it focused on his face.

Devereux flashed his badge and held it up to his eye. The eyepiece dilated again and the man turned away, focusing again on the youth at his door. Devereux took it as an informal welcome to the club. He stepped inside and a current of hot air met his face. The music was unbearable; it pounded into his head, drilling in the early symptoms of a wicked migraine.

There were two levels to the club. The first floor hosted the main stage where an orgy of men, women, and ambiguously-gendered people danced together in a storm of sweaty mist. The second floor hosted a smaller stage along with the DJ and his battery of instruments, keyboards, and amplifiers, stacked around him like a fort. Crimson light bathed the room, making the place even hotter. He unbuttoned his coat. It came as no surprise they called this place Hades; it was just a boiler room with laser light machines and music.

As he walked through the club he saw the show in full display. Sweat-soaked bodies grinded on one another in dance moves emulative of sex. No dialog exchanged lips, and even if it did, the words would be drowned out by the music's boom.

He shouldered past a couple of dancing men, bumping into their thrusting pelvises and swinging limbs. He swatted their arms away and pressed on.

Devereux turned away from the stage and walked toward the bar. He needed a clear vantage point. He brushed past a few inquisitive hands, groping and squeezing anything they could reach. As he approached the counter he patted his back pocket checking his wallet was still there.

A curvy redhead with smoky green eyes stared at Devereux as she leaned against the bar. She sucked on a red lollipop, slowly sliding it back in and out of her mouth, simulating fellatio. Her lips curved around the candy as her tongue licked up and down the tip. The drug was new but he recognized it instantly. The candy were colloquially known as *mollypops* on the streets. It was the invention of some Israeli kid who wanted to sneak drugs into a rave, so his rap sheet said. They were just lollipops laced with ecstasy but they were a hot seller and they had flooded dance clubs and classrooms everywhere.

Devereux stepped toward her. The girl leaned her head back, exposing her neck as she smiled at him. She blinked and her green eyes turned blue. She blinked again and her pupils became rainbow peppermints, her eyes engulfed in a swirl of colors. Devereux realized she wasn't smiling at him but enjoying the pleasures of an invisible world, all through the VR lenses of her contacts. He slid beside her and snatched the mollypop away. She kept smiling, nodding her head to the rhythm of the music, losing herself in the world of sound and color. He stomped on the mollypop. Hundreds of red pieces shattered under his feet like stained glass.

"Get you something, high roller?" a voice asked behind

him. Devereux turned. The bartender was a row of robotic arms spread along the length of the bar's counter with a virtual rendering of a man's face on a mobile LCD screen. A small camera atop the monitor shifted as it scanned Devereux. The image of the man shifted into the face of a brunette woman with long, dark lashes and full, red lips. She winked at him and bit her lower lip. Pattern recognition technology. He had only heard about it. Apparently, the camera could deduce someone's sexual preferences based on a number of factors such as retinal scans, social media history, body language and speech patterns. Devereux had never dabbled in social media and so, this monitor had concluded that Devereux was straight and preferred morally questionable brunettes.

"I'm looking for a man," Devereux said.

"Sorry, champ," the brunette on the screen said before morphing back to the man's face. "Got you all wrong. What'll it be?"

"No, I'm looking for the owner. Vincent Karpanian."

A few men sitting at the bar stiffened. Devereux looked around. They were men with hardened faces, all scars and wrinkles and downward curving lips. Men who had weathered the ugly storm of life. Not patrons. Undercover security. Probably ex-cons and veterans who still craved the adrenaline rush of a firefight. They eyed him, their hands hovered over their waists. Devereux shifted his coat, exposing his gun. He slid the holster's thumb break down and cocked the hammer. He slid the badge across the counter for the world to see. The weathered men growled, returning their gazes to their drinks.

"Sorry, Ace. He's back there," the man on the monitor said. A robotic arm swiveled and pointed towards a darkened corner of the room.

Devereux spotted what he was looking for. He nodded and walked away from the counter. Before he left, he heard the familiar voice of the brunette speak as another man took his spot against the bar. "Get you something, high roller?"

Karpanian was decked out in a slick Italian suit as he sat on a black leather couch against a wall on the furthest corner of the room. His slicked-back hair was probably doused in oils like the kids outside. He sported deep bags under his eyes, with a hooked nose, thick lips, and a cropped goatee. At his flanks, two large cronies in shades scanned the scene. They were Karpanian's organic surveillance cameras. Devereux wondered if they were augmented in some way, too.

Karpanian made eye contact with Devereux and whispered to his men. He chose the back corner like any good crime boss would've; you see everything, you know everything. *Power was forged in knowledge.* That was a common street credo he'd heard since he started his law enforcement career.

Devereux shoved and shouldered his way towards the V.I.P. area. A thick velvet rope separated the wealthy from the true players of the city: heads of industry, politicians, and studio executives. The real shot-callers mingled next to a group of scantily-clad women as they knocked back amber-colored liquid. What little clothes the girls wore were worth more than Devereux made in a year. They were probably nothing more than erotic sweatshop workers. Before leaving the cyber café, he had read the firsthand testimonies of a few call girls who said they used to work at a high-end ring out of Hades. They'd turned on Hades when they weren't getting paid their fair share. It amounted to a messy cycle. When money, sex, and drugs all changed hands, so did debt, death, and retribution.

The club was a familiar scene. Players changed, the game stayed the same. Audric Devereux had been a Vice detective for over a decade, now. Right out of high school and straight into the flames of the LAPD. As soon he logged his first five years on the beat, he'd applied for the position. Everyone dreamt about basking in the glory of Robbery or Homicide, but he knew the true corrosion of the city came from the vices that preyed on the poor, the disenfranchised. Drugs, gambling, and prostitution. He was surrounded by it as a child. And those three sins had a few things in common: they were easy to attain and they were affordable.

He eyed the freaks on the dance floor. Some moved with the grace of ballerinas dancing on silken clouds. Others jerked and swung their limbs like demons in battle. All were lost to the trance of banned stimulants in an attempt to fill some unfillable void. The void usually came at a steep cost: a chase that never ended. How many of these people had families left behind at home while they popped pills and chased tail? When you didn't care about yourself, your loved ones, what was the rest of the world to you? An ash tray? A mollypop playground?

The corrosion of the family unit. That was the root of it all. His family was torn apart by the evils of addiction, too. Devereux remembered the day his father had succumbed to an overdose, twitching on the bed, grasping at the sheets as his heart stalled and sputtered inside his chest like an old car. He left a single mother behind to raise two children inside a rotting guest house by the train tracks. And his brother, Robert, well, that was a travesty in itself.

Robert, his brother. The unfillable void. His own chase. The euphoric pipe dream, the unreachable nirvana. Night after night it went on with nothing to show.

The thing about drugs was that they burrowed themselves in the most seemingly safest of havens. Sanctuary was a myth. Drug pushers flooded parks outside of schools, trying to rake in new customers on the daily; boys who would grow up to get young girls pregnant only to overdose themselves, like his father. The cycle repeated itself. And as for the girls who needed money to raise their kids: prostitution never went out of business.

Damn you, Mom.
Bless you, Mom.

Vincent Karpanian had a smile on his face as Devereux approached. Tonight, he was the embodiment of all Devereux loathed.

"Would you like a drink of water, Mr. Devereux?" Karpanian shouted over the music. "I see you are sweating profusely. Or perhaps something a little more dangerous?"

"No. How do you know my name?"

"It might please you to know that your reputation is well-known."

Devereux shrugged. "Or your pet outside the door is sending you a live feed through his fancy eyepiece. I have a few questions for you, if you don't mind."

"I assumed you had questions when you walked through the door with a warrant, I presume?"

"I'm here as a civilian."

"So, you paid the entrance fee?"

He ignored the question and pulled out a notepad and a pencil with a worn eraser.

"Earlier tonight- "

"No PDA?"

"What?"

"You are using a pencil. Why?"

"Because," Devereux said looking into Karpanian's eyes, "Machines break down; codes become corrupted, triggering caches of memory dumps. As for the pencil; the story changes as it goes. People lie. Investigations are built on foundations of facts upon facts, only to find out later the facts were as sturdy as popsicle sticks. Pens make the lies permanent. A job like this, you find an eraser can be more important than a gun. Let's hope tonight we get our story straight.

Karpanian nodded to his two cronies. They walked ahead, leaving him alone with Devereux.

"Go," said Karpanian waving his hand dismissively.

"Earlier tonight, two men by the name of Gerald Cromwell, and his driver Samuel Beaudry Levine, were found murdered on Sunset Boulevard. An empty Magma cartridge was retrieved from Mr. Cromwell's car by our investigators. Witnesses reported seeing what appeared to be a young, Caucasian woman entering the car shortly before he died. She had thick, caked-on makeup and was wearing very little clothing. We believe she was a prostitute. In Mr. Levine's possession, I found a business card to Hades Nightclub."

"And this is one of your facts?"

"He was a low-wage driver. You run a club catering to hopped-up rich men and their sex-crazed children. He couldn't afford the ticket to an inferno like this. I'm gonna tell you what I already know. Levine came down here for his boss, picked out one of your call girls, and Cromwell took her for a drive. What I want to know is why one of your girls offed those two men?"

"You came here on a hunch, Detective? This isn't the old days, where the men in their fedoras hunted criminals down on intuition. So, you better fix your fucking tone before I get my attorneys involved."

He ignored the threat. "The Magma found in his car is an expensive narcotic only produced by expensive means; by the rich for the rich. I also happen to know you run a pharma-company out in Orange County. Diamorphine— ever hear of it?" Devereux smiled. "You are one crafty son of a bitch, Karp. Prostitutes and drugs, we know you got both."

"You can't prove a fucking thing," Karpanian said stiffening his shoulders in what Devereux assumed was anger. He started to push himself up off the couch.

Devereux put a firm hand on Karpanian's shoulder, sitting him down. He pulled out his phone. "You didn't even make this one hard, Vincent. One of the boys at the lab just sent me this." He swiped the screen with his thumb, clearing off the oily residue. He flashed it to Karpanian. It read:

'We just traced the Magma to Zylvan Corporation in Orange County. It's run by a Mr. Vincent Karpanian. Multiple complaints filed against Zylvan. We can get a search warrant approved as soon as you give the word. I think we got him.'

Karpanian sat upright. Yes, that hit a mark.

"The prostitutes. Talk."

Karpanian squirmed on his couch. He shook as he looked for his men. Devereux knew his type. If they weren't surrounded with lawyers, guards, or their entourage, they were just narcissistic crybabies, ready to crumble at the first sign of trouble. Paper tiger in a tie.

"Vincent. We know."

"I had nothing to do with any murder." A few beads of sweat trickled down his sideburns. He adjusted his shirt collar and looked away, breaking eye contact.

"I'll throw you a bone. Convince me and I might cool it on

looking too closely at your business tonight. You never know, maybe I'll forget. My short-term memory has been kind of screwy lately."

Karpanian turned his head slowly back to Devereux. "You're not here officially?"

"I'm just trying to catch a killer."

"Look, we might or might not run a high-end escort service. Some of our clients might also be inclined to send their errand boys or drivers to scope out the meat before they come in. But this girl," he shook his head. "She's not ours."

Devereux scribbled on the notepad. "How do you know?"

"All of our girls are here and accounted for. They've been here all night. No breaks. Full shifts."

Devereux gritted his teeth. "Cromwell. You know him?"

"No, never heard of him."

"He was Chief Financial Officer at Paradigm Industries."

"No. But a lot of those fuckboys from Paradigm like to party here. Just like the guys from Takashi Corp and Omnibank. They love this place. Besides, all the action happens only on our premises. That's the rule."

"Anyone in debt around here? Owe you money for services rendered or products sold?"

"No one gets anything without paying first. There are no debts in Hades. If you're here it's because you've bought your ticket."

Damn. Dead-fucking-end.

Devereux exhaled. Karpanian was dumber than he thought. That play was a gamble, but it worked. He had Walter Seamus from forensics send him a phony text; sometimes the only way to beat the rule breakers was to break a few yourself. But it looked like this trail had run head-on into a wall. He could always come back another day and nab Karpanian; it would be a cinch. But, tonight, a killer was still out there. He turned and walked way. He found if you didn't hurry, they faded right back into the shadows that spat them out.

He hoped homicide had made some progress on the Cromwell front. His eyes felt heavy. He needed to recollect his thoughts, gather the pieces.

Karpanian stood and followed behind. "So, we're good, right?"

"Tonight, your drugs didn't kill anyone," Devereux said. "Tomorrow might be a different story."

"So, you believe me?"

Devereux stopped and waved his pencil. "Let's just say I don't want to have to use this eraser."

He smiled and faded into the crowd.

***

CHAPTER SEVEN

THE TRAIN EXITED THE tube and rattled along the tracks summoning a hot breeze that scattered trash and debris. Its sleek steel frame lurched to a slow, creaky stop. The mechanical monster's doors hissed open, unloading its cargo of well-dressed flesh.

The wealthiest bodies in the business sector marched out in perfectly-pressed suits and neatly-cropped haircuts as they stepped on cracked concrete, past graffiti-blasted walls. Their shoes clicked and clacked on the floor like a herd of stampeding animals.

The businessmen who found the streets and highways too congested traveled within the underground system of veins and arteries of the subway. One of the popular transits among the well-to-do was the B Line. It weaved its way under prominent neighborhoods on the outskirts of the city and circled back downtown. It was a very exclusive line for the rich men who lived beyond the downtown epicenter of greed and gluttony.

This was the last stop. The Mulholland Drive station.

Lily leaned against a rusted wall. The fishnet stockings squeezed her thick, pale thighs all the way up to her short skirt. The black leather corset hugged her slender body and exposed the top of her breasts as they spilled out for the world to relish.

A scattering of perfectly-postured men stepped out. As they walked past her, they kept their heads down or pretended to look at their watches.

Lily smiled and winked at them anyway.

One man made eye contact with her. He was white, like most of the rest, and young. Lily smiled and winked again. He was attractive and had a bounce in his step reserved for the highly confident. His lips formed a mischievous half-smile. He made it a point to brush gently past her shoulder as he kept walking up the steps. A homeless man reached a hand out towards the young executive. The man walked passed him as if he were part of the dilapidated scenery like a dirty bench or a rusty turnstile.

Lily followed the man up the steps into the cold night. The rain had stopped but the clouds lingered as they veiled the moon. Lily followed the man a few paces behind. She was dreaming again. Things were slightly out of focus. The world had a bit of a haze around the edges, like the moisture eye drops usually caused. She knew the man, though she had never met him. Somehow her conscience told her his name was William Banks, thirty-five, and he was the Chief Operating Officer, and youngest member on the board at Paradigm Industries. Yes, she knew that. But how? She also knew Banks had a wife, same age, and two children, Bobby and Jacob.

Banks walked to a tree across the street and stopped under its shadow. Lily caught up to him and stopped at his back. Without turning, he said, "You're beautiful. And Asian. I'll bet you're really tight down there. How much?"

She thought she heard a faint whisper in her ear, like the distant crashing of ocean waves. "Cheap," Lily said without thinking, somehow just knowing it was the right thing to say. She looked at Banks' features. He was gorgeous and certainly he was wealthy enough to maintain that appearance. He had a perfect, square jaw and a nose that complimented his face, but she knew his nose was fake, and his jawbone had been chiseled and sanded down to his liking. Many actresses sought out this procedure to get a leg up, but fell shy of affording it. She always resented that. Though, truth be told, most of the wealthy took part in the procedures, trying anything to stave off imperfections or the effects of time. They were as plastic as their credit cards.

"My family is away this weekend. I never bring the meat home, but I'll make an exception this time. You're different. The makeup, your eyes. I like the outfit, too. Follow me but keep your distance. I'm not getting caught with a chink slut."

He walked up pristine streets with perfectly mowed hedges and tall, trimmed trees. Lily followed in shadows, pacing far behind. The suburbs were nothing like the city at all. The homes stood large and unafraid of their status, like proud men puffing their chests. She almost felt guilty walking by, like she didn't belong.

The leaves shuddered at the cold night's breeze, scraping against the asphalt. The temperature had dropped and Lily felt the cold wind blow up her skirt. She noticed, then, that she wasn't wearing underwear.

The longer she followed Banks, the more bizarre the dream felt. She tried to force herself to wake but the illusion persisted.

Banks came to a large iron gate and he punched in some numbers on a box. The gates parted for him and he waved her over. She crossed the threshold and walked beside him.

"You don't say much, do you? You speak English?"

Lily tried to say yes but shook her head instead. She knew she did, but the motion was instinctual like programing she couldn't break free from.

They followed a path of cobblestone inlaid on the grass. The house was big. It stood on a hill overlooking a valley of pinhole lights below. It had numerous balconies and looked about three stories large. The architecture was strange to her: a modern house with an unusually high ratio of glass to steel. All the windows were about five feet tall and hinted at the universe of comfort inside: the leather couches, marble countertops, intricate stereo systems. She walked past a window and saw her reflection. Her hair had been cropped a little shorter than usual and her makeup was heavy, caked on. Thick, inky eyeliner outlined her almond eyes. Neon pink lipstick coated her lips as they curved downward in a frown. She looked like a whore. Why was she dreaming about herself this way? Is this what her conscious was telling her about herself?

Banks punched in another code and a door opened. He grabbed her by the arm and escorted her inside. They walked past the living room with its polished hardwood floors and state-of-the-art entertainment system.

 William Banks held her hand and walked her upstairs. He led her to the master bedroom where a portrait of his two boys and wife watched silently as he kissed her lips. He held up his index finger as if to say wait, and walked to a small room she presumed was the bathroom.

 Lily felt ashamed to look around. The bed was huge and lined with pillows clearly of foreign import. The dressers were smooth and made of real wood, not that cheap, thin drywall stuff she had accidentally broken so easily on multiple occasions. The room was bigger than her apartment. She knew she didn't belong in a place like this. Nor would she ever.

 She heard heavy sniffling. Banks walked out with glassy eyes and the same mischievous smile. He walked up to her and leaned in. He kissed her, stopping every now and then to suckle gently on her lips. She felt dirty. It didn't feel right, but she couldn't open her mouth to say "no". Lily didn't know the man; he had never bought her a drink, or made her laugh, or whispered, "I love you," and meant it; but she couldn't resist. She wanted to wake up.

 Banks kissed her neck; his heavy breaths warmed her skin. This wasn't right. She wasn't a whore or a call girl for anyone's amusement. She just wanted to act and have people tell her she was great, that she was worthy of happiness, that she mattered.

 Strong hands gripped her corset and undid each lace one by one. Lily's breasts poured out. Banks buried his face in her neck. He grabbed her waist and pulled her in, their pelvises crashing into each other, fumbling over the buttons on his shirt with one hand as the anticipation coursed through him. With his free hand, he squeezed her breast. She wanted to push him off, but she couldn't. All she wanted was a fighting chance but her mind wasn't her own.

 Banks thrust her to the bed and smiled, pulling off her skirt slowly. He unzipped his slacks and took extra time removing his underwear, teasing her with what was to come. The room was dark but she saw his erection in the glimmer of moonlight.

He held his member in his hand like a murder weapon before releasing it and holding her wrists down against the bed.

"You're all mine now," he said.

Why was he doing this? She belonged to no one. Tears streamed down her eyes. She tried to push off his advance but found her arms only wrapping around his back. Her soul rejected every inch of William Banks but her body embraced it. She looked at her chest. The silver cross was gone.

"Oh, God," whispered Lily, as he entered her. She had never called upon any deity for help, she never felt she needed one, but she never felt as alone as she had now.

Banks rocked back and forth, pushing himself hard into her. Every stab hurt more than the last, the friction burning her insides.

The moans came from both their mouths, but Lily didn't recognize her voice as her own. She would never take pleasure in something like this. She tried again to push him away, but her hands only explored the man's back, tracing his shoulder blades with her fingers, almost pushing him into her with every thrust. Her mother would be ashamed. *But, Mother, it's not me...*

A migraine erupted. Her temples pounded and the world spun. William Banks looked surprised with his face awash in blue light. He tried to push himself off her body but she clasped her left hand around his neck and squeezed. Banks cocked his left hand for a punch, but Lily caught its onslaught in her free hand. She squeezed that too, and she heard the snap of small bones breaking like the crunch of dry leaves underneath boot heels. He tried to scream but all that came out was the sound of wet gurgling. Blood spewed from his mouth, splashing onto her hands. She tried to scream again but she could only clamp her teeth together. She wanted this to stop.

Lily loosened her grip and took her thumb and forefinger and ran it down his throat, feeling for the long tube. She squeezed her fingers together until her nails pierced skin as he bucked above her. Her other hand clasped around the back of his neck, keeping him in place while the fingers of her right hand closed around the meaty cylinder. She felt the fast, frightened pulse in her hand for a second. His eyes opened wide in disbelief as she ripped out his trachea.

The blood gushed over her breasts, the smell of it making her gag. She let go and pushed him off and Banks' corpse rolled off like a mannequin, its dead-weight hit the floor hard.

A wave of nausea flushed over her. Guilt shredded at her insides as if she had swallowed razor blades. Why was she here? This wasn't a dream. Her world had turned into a nightmare. She looked at her naked body. The man's juices glistened on her torso: blood, sweat, maybe even his semen. It could be wiped away, but the memory… it was inseminated inside; he was forever a part of her now.

Lily looked at the picture frame of Banks' family. In it, his wife and children looked straight ahead at the camera, smiling through white teeth. They hadn't helped. They were as silent to the deed as Lily had been. She wondered if they knew they were accomplices. She turned the picture face-down and grabbed her clothes. She ran out the premises of a building that was no longer a home.

***

CHAPTER EIGHT

HE HEARD THE SCREECHING and woke up with a muffled scream. A quick look around the darkness hadn't reassured him that it had only been a dream. In it, he was plugged into the cardiac monitor at the hospital. When he had heard the beeping, he thought his heart had flatlined and taken another plunge down Death Alley.

He had come home to gather himself. He'd closed his eyes and sleep had taken him. *Damn.* How long had he been out?

Devereux took a deep breath. He exhaled slowly and waited until his heart stabilized from the beating of the pistons in his chest. The doctors called it Hypertrophic Cardiomyopathy. In layman's terms, they told him his heart had thickened and he had developed chaotic heart valve function and it would have trouble pumping blood around his body. He tapped his left pectoral muscle and hoped his pacemaker was holding up fine.

He sat up and wiped the sweat from his brow. He looked around the room. The moonlight from the window above his bed illuminated the collage of faces to his left. Countless white cards lined the entire wall. They were the backs of junk mail ads; the ones that they sent every week with the pictures of missing children. Numerous little faces stared at him, their expressions from happier days frozen in a snapshot of wide, awkward smiles of missing teeth and juice-stained lips.

Their snapshots kept him going. They were the lost. He had an obligation to help them before they turned up as junk mail, destined for a trash heap somewhere. Or another wall like his. He couldn't help them all directly, but they were a reminder of the consequences; the trickle-down victims of vice.

He thought about Robert. The possibilities flew through his mind. Had he been kidnapped? Had he become a junkie? A criminal? Had any of those kids?

At best, they were runaways, lost to the streets and scooped up for the war effort. At worst…He heard the beeping again. The blinking red light on the vidbox told Devereux he had had a late-night call. He cursed under his breath and rubbed his eyes.

He sat up and faced the machine. "Answer," he said.

Kinneman materialized in front of Devereux's bed, wearing a mask of dark eye circles. A corkboard of notes and pictures told Devereux that Kinneman was still at the precinct. "Devereux, we got another murder for you."

"Don't do murders. I might consider doing you in though. What time is it?"

"Nine. Listen, Dev, we think it's in relation to the Cromwell case."

"Alright," Devereux said releasing a deep sigh, the fire in his chest starting to die down. "What've you got?"

Kinneman looked off-screen, his eyes shooting side to side as he read his PDA. "Uhm, William Banks, thirty-five. Chief Operating Officer at Paradigm. Lived on Mulholland Drive. Also, he's dead."

"Wait," Devereux said rubbing his temples. "Mulholland Drive?"

"Yup."

"How?"

"Trachea ripped from his throat. He bled out all over his bedroom floor. Neighbor called the police when he spotted a half-naked woman he didn't recognize fleeing the scene. There were trace amounts of cocaine on his clothing and we found him naked. Once again, nothing appears to be stolen."

"Naked?"

"Yup. Looks like he was getting his dick wet. We're running DNA tests super quick on this one. Hopefully we can score some positive ID's. Seeing a pattern here?"

"Paradigm, drugs, and hookers. And freakishly scary feats of strength."

"Looking like it. Banks' wife and kids were away visiting relatives. San Fran, I believe. We're trying to reach them for questioning."

"Mulholland Drive's at least twenty miles from Sunset. Someone's covering a lot of distance in a short span of time."

"Yeah. Looks that way. Traffic is ass-to-ass though. Don't know how the same person could've made Banks that quickly. Unless we're dealing with someone very committed. Maybe even multiple assailants. Anyway, we'll keep digging here. We're in communications with PD over there, until some of our guys can get there. Thought I'd keep you in the loop on this thing. Anything turn up on your end?"

Devereux thought about his off-the-books meeting with Karpanian. More and more it was looking like there was a strong bond between wealthy Paradigm executives and prostitution. Illicit drugs even. They all seemed to indulge in similar recreational activities. All of them happened to be married, too. Naughty. But Karpanian didn't seem to be involved, as far as Devereux could tell. He would stay true to his word and not burn his source. "Nothing solid yet. The string I pulled on led nowhere. I'll keep looking."

Kinneman's lip curved upward in an awkward grin. He shook his head. "You're losing it, Devereux. Guy like you would've had something by now." Kinneman chuckled to diffuse his passive-aggressive dig. Not slick. "Maybe, your heart's not in it anymore."

Devereux touched the scar on his chest. "Maybe you're right, Kinneman. Maybe you're right."

HE SWIPED HIS ACCESS CARD across his terminal. The green light blinked and LAPDOG greeted him coldly.

"Hello, Detective Devereux. This is LAPDOG. How may I assist you?" The screen turned green and a Nexus bubble popped up at its center.

"Computer, search William Banks, Paradigm employee.

Criminal history."

No Criminal History, popped up above Nexus. "Banks, William. No recorded history of crime or citations."

"Computer, check Paradigm for disciplinary actions against Banks."

A new bubble sprouted above the last. *Access Denied*. "That information is restricted to Paradigm Industries only."

Damn. LAPDOG granted access to virtually all public records and information. Corporations on the other hand, had special privacy privileges. They were the government sweethearts, bankrolling lobbyists, senators, anyone who had their hands in lawmaking. This guy Banks was good at keeping his record spotless. He did his sinning discreetly, in the comforts of his castle. If he had been a bad employee, there was no way to know. The cocaine was impossible to trace, and besides, Banks could afford anything he wanted. Like Cromwell, he probably didn't have any debts to square up. No, he didn't think it had anything to do with unsettled debts. What could it be?

Devereux rubbed his eyes and went over the facts in his head again. Two high ranking Paradigm employee's dead within hours of each other. And the driver. No, he was an unfortunate bystander. Had to be. Wrong place, wrong time, better luck next life. Nothing but a witness. Besides, he had nothing in common with the other two. Both were wealthy but nothing was stolen. Both married. Both abused substance. All died of broken necks, jaws, torn trachea's. Up close and personal. Raging strength. Rage. Was it punishment? Internal fighting? No. Everything was hazy. Nothing concrete. Think, Devereux. Hurry.

He stared at the digital LED clock on his monitor. The smallest hand ticked in a circle. *Time is just the unit of measurement by which we count something down towards its destruction.* His brother, Robert, had said that the night before he disappeared. The words were a truism Devereux had taken to heart on the job. As much a professional guideline, as a memento of the last thing his own flesh and blood had left him. He shook his head and kicked all thoughts of existential doom-and-gloom from his mind. His eyes felt heavy and wanted to collapse on themselves. *No. Stay awake.* He considered brewing a cup of coffee but thought better of it. The rapid-fire palpitations weren't worth the few extra minutes of alertness if it meant keeling over from a burst heart.

He closed his eyes. In that moment of weariness where the conscious and subconscious mind dance, another thought crawled into his brain. Not much but he had an idea.

"Computer, search Paradigm employees with public criminal backgrounds. Members of the Board."

Only one match. The name *Armand Belle* popped up. The only fool on the board not clever enough to clean his tracks. "Belle, Armand. Vice President, Paradigm Industries. Indicted on first-time charges of soliciting, two years prior. Charges dropped in exchange for a fine and community service."

Bingo. He was hot out of solid leads. No facts. Just a guess. If he was a betting man, he'd slap some cash on a wager that Mr. Belle was about to have his throat wringed. Or torn out. Whichever came first.

"Computer," Devereux said as he reached for his coat. "Get me Belle's address."

***

CHAPTER NINE

COLD HANDS TRACED THE outline of her face. Rough fingers gently slid down her cheeks, reassuring her like she remembered her father doing when she was just a child, before he left his family to start a new life someplace else.

Lily felt drained. She was tired of the nightmares. And the pain. In between her legs, her insides felt as if they were doused in fire. Then came a pounding in her head, uncontrollable and wild. She opened her eyes. The darkness was there, waiting for her. She turned her head and heard the faint breaths of what sounded like a man. Her eyes adjusted. The red light of the terminal's screen lit the room. A shadow hovered over her face and moved away. The silhouette of a man stepped beside her, watching.

She brought her arms to her chest and felt bare skin. She was naked again.

"You've been a good girl, Lily," a coarse voice said. "You're doing a great job. And don't think that God hasn't noticed."

She felt chills, like a million tiny spiders crawling on her skin. All the short hairs on her body stood on end. The man plunged a needle in her neck. She felt cold fluid coursing through her veins.

"This is Delirium in its liquid form. It's going to make you feel like you're dreaming. It'll ease the pain." He removed the syringe. Lily eased her arms and they fell to her sides.

Lily turned to the man, his face was obscured by the shadows. Her senses started to dull and the muscles in her limbs relaxed. She felt the moisture of tears well in her eyes. She blinked and little rivers streamed down her face.

"You don't have to be scared of me. I'm here to facilitate your entrance into paradise. Think of me as your spiritual counselor, your priest." He laughed. "Are you ready to confess your sins?"

Lily turned and shut her eyes. The man slid his fingers through her hair, gently twirling a few strands.

"It's alright. You don't need to speak. None of them ever do, anyway."

He retrieved a small black case. With one hand, he held her chin, and with the other, he applied a coat of lipstick on her mouth. She squirmed as much as her body would let her, but he tightened his grip. A bolt of pain traveled through her face that the drugs couldn't numb. He could've easily crushed her jaw if he wanted to. When he was done, he caressed her face gently again.

"Very pretty," he said in a low, gravelly voice. He took a deep breath and exhaled, the warm air touching her face. "This world is falling apart all around us, Lily. I know you see it. It's become morally bankrupt. War, drugs, politics. We have become unworthy of life. We've become an incurable virus. Corrupted lines of code. Our only salvation is ascension. Unfortunately, that means leaving the world of flesh and bone behind. We have to set things right by punishing those most responsible for this malady."

He stepped away and sunk into the shadows. Her eyes felt heavy. She was going to black out again. The rumble of a car engine came to life. A flood of white light filled the room. It burned Lily's eyes.

"I don't know how long you have to live," he said walking into the light.

His silhouette became black amongst the light and took on a twisted, disfigured form. It's as if the light spat out a living shadow man. A boogeyman. Lily pressed her eyelids shut. She squeezed them until it hurt.

"The others didn't last long. Most of them never made it past the experimental stage. But you, you're strong." He reached for her. "You're my favorite."

Mother. Mother, Help me.

***

CHAPTER TEN

DEVEREUX STRUGGLED TO KEEP his eyelids open. He hadn't had a night this long since his first year as a beat cop, back when he'd strained adjusting to those long graveyard shifts they tossed young bloods like him.

He hoped this worked, it was really all he had left. It amounted to good, old-fashioned police work. No computers, no Nexus. Just a gut feeling and the will to power through it. The trail had begun to dry up along with the rain that brought it in. In his line of work, if you couldn't find it, you let it find you. He had learned that lesson spending countless hours shadowing dealers and pornographers as they wallowed in their depravity.

He pulled his unmarked Interceptor into a no-park zone across the street from Paradigm Tower and killed the engine. He waited.

Devereux had driven to Belle's listed address. It was a high-rise condo up on Bunker Hill. All sparkly glass and potted plants and snobs who couldn't be bothered to look you in the eye to say 'hello'. He had flashed his badge to the woman working the front desk. She had smiled and buzzed him past the electrically sealed doors. He checked the garage for the parking space that pertained to Belle's residence. Nothing but an empty space. In the space, next to it, a large, black minivan sat idle in a light coat of dust.

Devereux had gone to Belle's condo and knocked. A woman with short, blonde hair greeted him. She looked worn and weary. The woman might have once been beautiful and the object of men's desires. Now, she had stood in a slight slouch like a revenant woken from its tomb.

"Can I help you?" she had asked.

"I'm looking for your husband," Devereux had said as he reached for his badge.

She answered him before he even pulled it out. "He said he was staying out late at the office. Some big board meeting tonight. Paradigm. Goodnight." She slammed the door.

For all she knew he was a contract killer. Didn't seem to matter to her one way or the other. Devereux presumed Belle wasn't up for the Husband of the Year award.

This was the end of the line now. Devereux looked out his car window. Paradigm Tower, where men came to play God as they merged man and machine behind smoky-tinted windows. The building was clean and immaculate, like a castle fit for modern-day deities. Concrete, glass, and steel. Its windows were living broadcasts of reflections of all who walked past. The building reminded you of what you were and weren't. If you were a suit-and-tie man, you knew it; if you were a rag-mummy, it let you know that, too. Beyond the life of the skyscrapers and all who worked inside was the life of the peasants who toiled in the streets and sixteen-hour work shifts. Like him.

Devereux worked out the angles in his mind while he waited. Why were these men murdered? As for a motive, it was possible that it was economic. But a call girl gaining intimate access to prominent men from the same company? Odd. There was no evidence that money was taken, and the men weren't extorted. Sure, they had secrets, but nothing a quick divorce and a new wife wouldn't patch up. They all abused substance but he didn't know if that was the connection. They had enough money to not piss off a dealer. No, that wasn't it.

His mind circled to something he had toyed with earlier. Internal fighting. They were all members of the board. They must've been pretty close, known each other's ticks, pleasures, et cetera, et cetera.

A blue luxury sedan pulled out from the belly of the garage. He caught a glimpse at the plates. Devereux checked his notebook and confirmed it belonged to a Mr. Armand Belle, Vice President of Paradigm Industries. Devereux started his engine and followed.

The sedan was a new model; off the lot, factory sticker kind of new. The dick-rocket was a sleek and sporty two-seater. The kind of car a man owns who likes to bring a single passenger along for the evening. It looked promising.

He shot a look at his clock. It read 10:30 pm. The cold weather had come crawling in to stay like a strung-out squatter. Devereux cranked up the heater. It made a clunking noise and blew out cold air and dust. Damn. Broken. He ignored it.

Belle rocketed through the streets past a series of red lights, narrowly avoiding a few pedestrians. His engine roared as Devereux struggled to keep pace in his outdated Interceptor. Belle ditched the lights of Downtown and swerved through curvy residential streets and beatnik districts. A scattering of vagabonds and dealers still stalked the sidewalks, but for the most part, the streets were empty. The big crowds had abandoned the suburbs and moved toward the heart of Downtown, flooding the streets like an electric carnival.

Belle drove to a rundown neighborhood in Echo Park, where the beatniks, artists, and homeless rubbed shoulders, sometimes indistinguishably. The blue sedan stopped across the street from a watering hole. Devereux parked down the street and killed his lights. The bar was called *The Emporium*, and groups of drunken youths lingered around the entrance chatting and smoking cigarettes. Nothing unusual except for the fact that Belle never stepped foot out of his car.

A pair of ugly women in short skirts approached Belle's window. Devereux gripped the wheel. After some small talk, they moved on down the street. Devereux jotted down the address to reference a possible prostitution spot.

The knock on Devereux's window startled him. A man in tattered clothing smiled and pointed his finger downward. Devereux lowered the window. He regretted it immediately. The man reeked of old clothes that had been soaked in urine and left out to dry.

"Hey man, you need *drogas*?"

"Not interested," Devereux said shifting his eyes between

the bum and Belle's car.

"I've got Coke, Valium, you name it. Mollypops for the kids."

Devereux whipped his badge out and waved it side to side. "Not. Interested."

"Oh, you're probably into those new cyber drugs. Well, I ain't got 'em. Shoot, what you think this is? Silicon Valley?" The man shoved his hands in his pockets and limped away.

Devereux returned his gaze to the bar. He watched as the influx of youth slowed to a trickle. No one matching the murderer's description ever showed her face. After an hour, the blue car pulled away and cruised up the street. Devereux turned the ignition, waited five seconds, and followed, making sure to stay two cars behind. Belle slowed every time a girl walked by; Black, White, Hispanic. The bastard was seeing what was on the menu.

The girls huddled together when Belle pulled up beside them, shrugging off his advances like he was another beggar on the street. Belle wasn't discerning between prostitutes and girls out to have a good time. He was thirsty.

Belle cut a sharp right and pulled into the shadow of an alley. Devereux parked and stepped out. The wind pulled at his clothes. His chest constricted and he pulled his coat in tight. He stepped towards the alley and peered over the wall. A woman leaned into Armand Belle's window. She was short but he couldn't make out much more than that.

A few minutes dragged by and the woman disappeared inside the sedan. Belle killed the lights. Naughty time. Devereux walked ahead and tapped the holster at his hip for reassurance.

The car began to rock rhythmically as he approached. A gust of wind blew through the alley and howled like a wounded beast, masking his footsteps as he approached. Devereux stared at his own reflection as the tinted windows obstructed his view inside. He looked back. His car was behind the corner, at the entrance of the alley. If he needed backup, he would be far from calling it in. *Screw it.*

He approached the driver-side door and tapped on the

window. "Sir, this is the LAPD, are you alright in there?"

No answer. Devereux knocked again. "Can you please lower your window? I'd like to speak with you."

A blue light shone inside. He took a step back and snapped his holster's thumb break down. A moment passed. He wrapped his hand around the butt of his pistol. The touch of steel almost didn't register as his fingers had numbed from the cold.

Armand Belle's head crashed through the driver's side window in an explosion of glass. The skin of his face and neck became caught in the serrated shards of glass as blood splattered onto Devereux's coat. Belle's eyes stared lifelessly at the asphalt floor.

A woman stepped out of the passenger door. Her eyes were blue lights, shining in the dark of the alley. She was short and light-skinned. She wore fishnet stockings and a tight corset. Her face was powdered white like the descriptions from before. She resembled a horrifying sado-masochistic doll.

Devereux drew his pistol and aimed it at the woman's head. "Police! Turn around and place your hands on your head!"

The woman walked towards him. The blue lights hovered like orbs as she stepped closer. He put up a hand to shield his eyes from the brightness. Devereux took a step back, glanced at Belle's body, and then back to her. Beads of sweat trickled down his forehead.

His heart pounded inside his chest. His pacemaker was drawing electric interference, throwing his palpitations out of sync. How? He breathed short, violent gasps as the woman walked forward. His hand trembled as he raised it for a shot but the living doll snatched it and squeezed. A sharp burst of pain erupted in his hand like he was palming hot coals. He let go of the gun. Her other hand was on his neck before the gun hit the floor.

He stared into the blue lights as the woman lifted him off the ground and slammed him against Belle's car. A jolt of pain exploded through his back.

He grabbed her fingers and tried to pry them loose. They

were locked solid. His windpipe constricted, cutting off his air flow. Black spots filled his eyes and lethargy weighed on his limbs as they started to go numb. He turned to look at Belle again, his head in the vice of the window's glass teeth. Devereux reached over, buried a shard in his grip and squeezed. His hand bled as he twisted back and forth, snapping a fragment loose. He swiped the glass across the woman's face, spraying Devereux with warm blood. Her grip loosened. He twisted her wrist, breaking him free as he fell to the floor on his knees. He screamed as the pain pulsed up his bones.

Devereux saw his pistol as it lay in a puddle of water. He reached for his sidearm, but she was too fast. She kicked the pistol away before his fingers could curl around the handle. Devereux shoulder-rolled forward and snatched the pistol barrel-first in his bloodied hand. It felt heavy. The palm of his hand burned as his fingers squeezed the gun. *Come on. Move.*

She stepped toward him, fingers curling into fists. She drew her arm back and fired off a punch. With what little strength he had, he spun around and ducked, narrowly avoiding the blow.

She cocked for another swing. He bent his legs, and pushed off like a wound coil. Devereux swung his arm, bearing down the full weight of the butt across her temple. Her legs buckled before giving out. She collapsed on the street, her skull striking asphalt in what sounded like a wet crunch.

Devereux sucked in a deep breath and coughed uncontrollably. The liquid in his mouth tasted like rusted pennies. He leaned against the door of the sedan and tried to steady his breaths. He coughed some more, stopping only to spit out blood. After a few minutes his heartbeat normalized and the fire in his chest started to die down.

He turned to look at Belle and then returned his gaze on his killer. The blue lights faded as she lay in a puddle of water and blood. He wasn't sure whose it was; maybe all of theirs.

Devereux took a seat on the floor. He wondered if he had died and gone to hell. Their killer was a prostitute with light-emitting eyes and freakish strength. Good luck radioing that in.

He'd seen some crazy shit before- hell, he'd worked Hollywood- but this one was a head-scratcher.

He pulled out his notepad. He stared at the thin red lines on the paper, and for once, he wasn't sure what to write. He spat out more blood, got up, and walked to his car.

***

CHAPTER ELEVEN

THE NIGHTMARES CAME AGAIN in a torrent of flashes and hazy snippets. It almost felt like those nights on the couch when she would fall asleep to a bad horror movie on the Holoscreen. She saw a grimy city with grimy people, where even the buildings looked menacing. And the feeling of other men's hands on her, entering her privates. It made her shiver. She had seen her hands tear a man's throat out as a cascade of blood poured out on the floor. She remembered shoving another man's head through a car window. Images of a shadow man caressing her face.

And the man in the coat. In her dream, she felt cold and wet. She remembered being lifted off the ground and seeing his face. His hands were on her, but she didn't feel afraid then. He whispered something to her she didn't quite understand, but she nodded anyway. Whatever it was, the words held no malice or deceit behind them.

Her eyes opened; the lights burned. After a while her eyes adjusted, and things started taking form; white walls, blue sheets, strange electrical apparatuses. Tubes pierced her arm and cold nodes clung to her limbs and torso. *No. Not again.*

A deep throbbing burst in her temples, pounding rhythmically to the beat of her heart. She shook her head and saw something move. She sat up and clenched her fists.

An old man wearing a white lab coat walked in, looked at her and smiled. His hair was a nest of tangled, wiry hair, some of it in messy coils. He fidgeted with his glasses as he slouched over a computer monitor beside her. He nodded and left the room. A few moments later, he walked back in with two other men. The first through the door was a man in a black shirt and rolled up sleeves; it looked like he hadn't shaved or slept in days. He was a man of average height and build, with short hair and dark eyes. He wore a face of concern, like a parent picking up a child from the school nurse. The other walked in last. He was tall and lean with broad swimmer's shoulders. He had blue eyes and dark blonde hair. An unlit cigarette dangled from his lips.

"Welcome back, Ms. Santos," the unshaved man with the dark eyes said. He pulled up a seat and sat next to her.

Lily looked at him quizzically. "Welcome back where?"

"To the land of the living."

Lily didn't respond. She let the statement sink in. For a while the only sound was the beeping of the machines.

"You were unconscious. You suffered a concussion that knocked you out cold."

"How?"

"I smashed the butt of my gun on your head. I'm Detective Audric Devereux, by the way." He gently placed a hand on her shoulder. "And this," he said nodding to his tall friend, "is Detective Michael Kinneman."

Kinneman nodded. "The wound isn't anything to worry about," he said. "It didn't cause any major damage."

Lily's hand felt for the wound. She touched a bump on the top of her head. Her head. Lily's face contorted as a memory crept its way into her conscious. Her hand slid towards the back of her skull and felt cold metal. She mouthed the word 'No', and looked at the men for answers.

Detective Devereux looked at the man in the white coat. "Doctor Samuels will fill you in. He's one of the leading neurosurgeons in the country."

The doctor adjusted his glasses and cleared his throat. He was nervous about something. "Ms. Santos, I don't know how to say it, so I'll just go ahead and tell you. When we brought you to the hospital, we examined your head wound and found some anomalies. We took a closer look and, well, this may be disturbing."

Lily took a deep breath. She gripped the sheets and closed her eyes as she waited for the words to fall, like an executioner's axe.

"We found a small metallic shunt on the back of your skull, about the size of a quarter. We also found steel bulges running down the length of your spine. We took some x-rays and, well, Ms. Santos, someone has performed some very complicated invasive procedures."

The nightmares. They were real? Her stomach twisted itself into intricate knots. Her breathing began to quicken as the adrenaline of fear kicked in. She wanted to throw up in the worst way. Her hand reached for her chest, but the cross was gone. She felt naked, exposed.

Devereux crossed his arms around his chest and looked at the floor. Kinneman bit his cigarette and nodded.

Doctor Samuels continued. "It appears you have undergone experimental neural procedures. Mind control procedures, to be exact."

Devereux leaned in. He awkwardly clasped his hand over hers. The man wasn't very good at this. He squeezed. The feeling almost didn't register.

"This might sound a little complicated," Samuels said, "but bear with me." He looked over the PDA in his hands. "There is a protein in green algae, called Channelrhodopsin, that when exposed to the spectrum of blue light, causes positive ions to fire into local cells. This protein was synthesized and infused into a virus that was then injected into your brain through this shunt here," he said taking a pen, pointing it at the back of her head. "This virus infected your neurons and delivered the gene deep into your brain tissue. Now, there are implants embedded behind your eyes, through use of fiber optics, which shine blue lights directly into your brain. This releases the protein, causing synapses to fire, releasing neurons that affect particular behaviors such as aggression, or fear-"

Which, Devereux realized, is why he saw her eyes glowing blue.

"When the neurons fire," continued Samuels, "they relay electrical impulses down the spine and nervous system. That is where a separate mechanical device was implanted into your spine. The implant collects the synapses and transfers them to your limbs for better control of your body, which was used in questionable ways." He cleared his throat again and swallowed. "We also found your hands and forearms have been surgically removed and augmented with advanced prosthetics. These augmentations are powerful enough to crush steel. I know it's hard to tell, but the synthetic skin grafted onto your arms is nearly identical to the real thing. It even registers touch and sensation, though I assume not at the same sensitivity."

Lily shook her head. She didn't understand. She had never heard these words, these complicated terms. And now they came flooding in like a typhoon. *Augmentations? Mind control?* What were these men trying to say? Where was her mother? Where was her agent? Anyone? As she stared at the strangers in front of her, she realized she was alone.

Samuels continued, "As well as having optical fibers in your eyes, whoever performed these surgeries implanted a BCI, or Brain Computer Interface, which is a direct communication pathway between the brain and an external device or receiver. They attached a neurotropic electrode to your thalamus, which decodes signals from the retina. In other words, you had a visual transmitter in the back of your eyes which relayed all you saw to the receiver."

"Meaning," Kinneman added shifting the cigarette in his mouth, "someone out there was using you to do their dirty work, and they could see, and possibly hear everything you did."

"Dirty work? What did I do? I don't remember. What's going on? Please, someone tell me what happened."

Devereux took a breath. His brows shifted as he searched for words. He didn't know what to say.

Kinneman took a few steps forward and plucked the cigarette out of his mouth. "Four men have been murdered tonight. Their deaths were similarly executed and occurred over the span of just around five hours over the Los Angeles Metropolitan area. With the first two murders, witnesses reported seeing a tall, blonde woman fleeing the scene of the crime on foot. The third murder, a witness told police he saw a short, dark haired woman leaving the premises of the scene. The fourth, well," Kinneman said pausing as he searched for words. "Here you are."

Lily stared blankly at the wall. "I've been having bad dreams. I've seen ugly things. Like I was sleepwalking. Nightmares I couldn't wake from. I killed people. But they were just dreams. Right?"

"It's not your fault, Lily," Devereux said. "You're going to be cleared of any wrongdoing. We can prove this wasn't your fault."

She closed her eyes for a moment and imagined Devereux's hand being her mother's. Except her mother's hands were warm, and this man's hands felt cold, impersonal.

"But," Kinneman said, "we don't know who did this to you, and why. We know there was the other girl. Your description doesn't match up with the first suspect. Our mastermind might be snatching up other women. Who knows what he can do? We're currently tracking down every possible lead. We're piecing together all the patterns in the deaths of the victims. But, quite frankly, we need your help in capturing him."

Her eyes welled, the moisture collecting on the bottom of her eyelids; she closed them and the tears finally came. "How did I kill them?"

Samuels looked at the detectives. They said nothing.

"*How?*"

"You sure you don't remember?" Devereux asked.

The question stung. Did they not believe her? Weren't they supposed to be on her side?

"Tell me," she said finally.

"We're still waiting on the official cause of death from the coroner's office, but your DNA was found at the scene of one Mr. William Banks' home on Mullholland Drive. His trachea appears to have been torn out of his throat. The second death occurred in my presence. That was Mr. Armand Belle. You smashed his head against his car window, severing his throat against the glass."

She felt her temples throbbing, the sound of blood

coursing through her head as her face flushed. She remembered the pain in her privates. "Did those men touch me?"

"Your body was used to bait certain prominent men, and-"

"I was raped."

"Yes." Devereux squeezed her hand tighter. She thought she felt it this time.

Lily turned away. The tears felt cold streaming down her face. She moved a finger to wipe them away but the moisture didn't register. She looked at her fingers. Lily wiggled them individually in front of her face. They weren't hers.

She gasped for air as she sobbed. "I want these implants off me. I want to go home," Lily said. "I have an audition tonight. I need to get that role."

"I'm sorry," Samuels said. "We have to keep you here for monitoring." He turned his face away.

"I don't want to be here. Can't you take these things off me?"

Devereux lowered his head apologetically. Lily imagined it was the same rehearsed look he had to give family members of the recently-deceased. "Lily, I'm not sure how to say this, but there are complications. The spinal implants have fused to your tissue. There's a vast network of nerve connections and we don't know how your body will react. There is good news. The BCI emits radio signals to the receiver, but they got weaker over time as your brain developed scar tissue over them. Whoever our guy is, he can't see you anymore. The bad news, Lily, is that your brain is rejecting the foreign objects in a bad way. You might experience severe migraines as time goes on."

"What are you trying to tell me?" She said clutching her sheets like a security blanket.

"We don't know if you have long to live," Samuels said.

Her throat felt dry as she swallowed a hard lump. Her heart sank into a gulf of black. That's the only she could describe it. Like staring at the ocean at night. An infinite void.

"I know it's hard to take," Kinneman said. "Finding this man is the only way we can help you now. These are advanced surgical procedures, and he may be the only one who can undo this. You have to tell us what you remember. Who picked you up? Where did they take you?"

She almost didn't hear the questions from the pounding rhythm of a new migraine. She looked up, scanning all three men. She could barely see them through the thin film of tears, newly formed over her eyes. Even those weren't wholly hers. "What am I?" She asked.

"I'm sorry, ma'am?" Kinneman asked.

"These things," she said sliding a hand over her forearms, "These implants. They're not me. They're not real."

Devereux stood and stepped closer. He looked her over. Lily saw a man struggling to speak, as his face became a portrait of confused anguish. He bit his lower lip as he searched for words. A poet, Lily assumed, he was not. He unbuttoned his shirt. A thin white scar ran vertically down his bare chest. Devereux traced the scar with his middle and index finger.

"My heart hasn't pumped a drop of blood on its own in over ten years. And it's only getting worse. I have a degenerative condition. I'm doomed. But, as we speak, I have a machine inside me. It sends little shocks to my heart, every second of every day. Keeps it pumping. It's the reason I'm alive. Nothing else. I stand too close to a microwave; I get a heart attack. I were to run a lap, I'd drop before the finish line. Anything distresses its delicate little rhythm: booze, smokes, coffee, scary movies, and it all goes away. I'm at the mercy of technology, but my shortcomings, my differences, my implant, those don't define me. I define me. There is nothing fake about me, Lily. I'm as real as this night has been scary. And right now, I need you to help me catch a killer."

She closed her eyes and drew a deep breath. The realization hit hard. A death sentence. Borrowed time. Is this what Mother felt like, knowing she had cancer, keeping quiet as it festered inside her, gnawing away at her insides day by day? Was it shame that made her keep the truth from Lily? Whatever it was, it was a secret that thrived inside its host until its last breath was drawn. *Why didn't you tell me, mom? I could've helped. Could've.*

She thought about the other women; the ones to come still.

No.

I. Can. Help.

She closed her eyes and took a breath, letting the cold hospital air settle in her lungs. She opened her eyes. "I only remember dirty walls, tubes, wires. And other women."

Devereux scrambled for his notepad. He slashed his pencil across paper, scribbling up a frenzy while Kinneman jabbed his PDA, his fingers typing up a flurry of notes. "Can you describe the girls?" Devereux asked. "Can you describe them for me, Lily?"

She scanned the floor as the memories trickled in. Images of bloated bodies and pale faces staring dumbly at the floor took shape again. She pulled her knees close to her chest. What she thought were nightmares was reality. What was reality she wished were nightmares. "Yes. I can describe them." She paused to swallow. The onset of cottonmouth. The men waited on her words like eager children. She massaged her right temple with her index and middle finger. "One woman was blonde, I think. She was young. The other, I can't remember too well. Dark hair. Older."

"That's great, Lily," Devereux said. "Are there any other details you can remember? Were they hurt?"

"They're dead," she said looking away. "All of them are dead." She buried her face in her knees and sobbed.

Devereux looked up from his notepad and stared at Kinneman, who had nearly chewed through his cigarette. Samuels grimaced. Devereux turned to the clock on the wall. Two in the morning. The gears clanked loudly, the hands seemingly moving faster than normal, counting down towards destruction. He looked back at Lily, her muffled sobs filling the room. Everything was destined to break down; that was the way of things. Finality. Borrowed time. The trick was knowing how to make the best of it while you had it.

Devereux clasped Kinneman's shoulder. "We need to move quick. He'll want to replace Lily with someone else soon."

The men moved toward the door.

She thought about her mother's cancer again, as the men neared the door. Cancer, the doctors had told her when her mother passed, was classified as an abnormal growth of cells. The tainted cells then spread and spread until they interfered with the body's routine functions. Unchecked, the disease replicated itself, growing exponentially until either it was destroyed, or its host was. Lily wiped her face. The man who operated on her was a cancer. He didn't care about her or the other women. And he would continue to do it, tainting more and more people, until… She didn't know. Did evil have limits?

She pulled the sheets from her body and pushed herself off the bed. She tore the nodes and IVs off her body. She stood there facing the men in her hospital gown, traces of drying tears still on her cheeks.

"Get me some clothes," she said, a tinge of fire in her voice. She was surprised the words had come out of her mouth. "I'm coming with you. If I'm going to die, I might as well help you make sure no one else does."

***

CHAPTER TWELVE

SHE SAT TOWARDS THE back corner of the room, her fingers tapping on the table. She was agitated, impatient, nervous; he wasn't sure which. The briefing room was empty, and the few officers on duty hadn't looked twice as they walked her in. Even the Night Watch Commander was indifferent as he strode past them in the hallway.

Devereux looked back at her. She was an enigma. Just a few hours ago she had tried to kill him. Just a few moments ago she had been crying, knowing soon, her life could end soon. Now, she was here with them. Offering to help any way she could.

Samuels had protested her leaving the hospital but she had been right. She didn't have long to live. Hell, she was the only person who had any useful information locked somewhere in her head. Devereux told Samuels there would be no harm in her tagging along. At least until her memory returned. Or until they got caught.

Kinneman chewed on a cigarette as he looked at his watch. He'd helped Devereux sneak her into the precinct. She had given him her size and he had returned with clothes rummaged from the precinct's lost-and-found department.

Devereux turned away from Lily and flipped his notepad open. Its insides were marked with chicken-scratch notes, sketches, and the faint smears of words that couldn't be erased. Countless months of casework and interviews, all on hardcopy. "Alright let's take it step-by-step."

Kinneman swiped his card across the terminal and the Nexus sprang up, filling the entirety of the front wall. He cleared the podium away and walked back to Devereux.

Henry Samuels stepped inside the room, carrying a tray of coffee cups. On his chest hung a 'visitor' badge on his lanyard. Kinneman swooped up a cup and sipped it hot. The doctor placed a cup on the table where Lily sat. She forced a smile. Devereux waved off the offer and scanned his notepad.

Kinneman put the coffee on the table. "Alright, gentlemen. And Ms. Santos. We know that a lot of women have been reported missing this month. We can't go over each individual case and look at their last known whereabouts or form any kind of pattern in the amount of time we have. We don't know which, if any of them, our mastermind has kidnapped. The clock's ticking. Where do we point the magnifying glass?"

"The implants. We break it down piece by piece," Devereux said. "Tech by tech. We treat it like any other case. Follow the breadcrumbs, see where it goes."

"Yes," Samuels said. "The technology used on Miss Santos was very particular. Unique, even."

"Alright, whadda we got?" Kinneman asked.

"Let's start with the virus," Devereux said. "Doctor Samuels, is it possible to track this thing down?"

"Well, yes, but there are quite a few labs in the States working with the algae that produces it. It's a common biological specimen, though the experiments never reached anything past testing on mice. This is something beyond my expertise. Most of the testing facilities are on the East Coast."

"Computer," said Devereux. "List all federally or privately funded labs that have samples of-" He turned to Samuels.

"Channelrhodopsin, computer," Samuels replied.

Nexus shot a line upward and formed a new bubble called *Laboratories*. A large group of smaller bubbles formed beside it, listing the names of all the laboratories in the country that met the search criteria.

Damn. "Computer, reference same laboratories for reports of theft or sabotage."

No Reports, read the new bubble.

"Might take all night to call them up and ask who they've

delivered to," Kinneman said.

"There's gotta be something we can use to figure this out quickly."

Devereux flipped a page on the notepad. "The implants. All the electrical apparatuses and fiber optics. The BCI."

"Those," sighed Samuels. "Those, anybody with a basic knowledge in electronics could have soldered and pieced together at home. The key here is the precision of the surgery itself. The knowledge of anatomy. It is of an expert level. We're looking at someone who has a proficient knowledge in electronics and biology. Too broad to narrow down. I'd have to make calls to colleagues, see who meets the criteria. That could take a while."

"That leaves the prosthetics," said Kinneman picking up his coffee again. "Those hands, the arms. Military grade. There's a very specific company that excels at that and," he said turning to Devereux, "I know you're thinking the same thing." He sipped his coffee in triumph as if he had just scored a breakthrough. "We don't have a motive but the murders can't be a coincidence. Paradigm."

Devereux let out a sigh. Kinneman was right. He knew there'd been a strong connection waiting to be explored there. But the maze of red tape ahead was looking impossible to cut through. "We don't have enough to dig up a warrant," Devereux said. "And we can't legally access their database to compare the tech. Might be top secret stuff. Have we been in touch with them tonight?"

"Yep," Kinneman said. "They're cooperating with the investigation. Say they're sorry to hear the news; they were good men, blah, blah, blah. But something's not right, Dev. Three high-ranking Paradigm men offed all gruesome in one night. Sounds to me like someone's overdoing it on the severances."

"There might be something else," Samuels said. He walked to the back corner and pulled up a chair beside Lily. She stiffened in her seat. Samuels put his hands up as a gesture to show no ill-intent. She eased up. He raised her right arm gently, turning it over slowly. He traced his fingers across her synthetic skin. She looked puzzled as her eyes furrowed slightly. "This skin. It's cutting edge. Not like any other artificial skin. Collagen Polymer. And only one company makes it. Dermalab. Company out of Oakland. I haven't dealt with the polymer in my operations personally, but I have performed surgery on patients with substantial amounts of brain damage. These patients typically have extensive facial injuries and are either military personnel or civilians involved in critical work accidents. Those who can afford it go on to receive facial reconstruction surgeries using the artificial skin. The prosthetic is nearly unidentifiable from real organic tissue."

"Bingo," Kinneman said. "Lily said there were other girls. Whoever was doing this must've needed lots of this stuff. We can check bulk shipments, check who they've been delivering to. Maybe pull some names out of Los Angeles."

"They're a private company. We can't access that information either," said Samuels. "They'll never cooperate or reveal who they've done business with."

"We need something admissible in court. Something to show a judge," Devereux said. "Some kind of hardcopy evidence or even data from their mainframe." As the words rolled off his tongue, something sparked in his mind. He rifled through the pages in his notepad. He stopped flipping when he found it. "I've got an idea. Something from my last case."

Kinneman looked weary as he sipped his coffee. The bags under his eyes were dark and his frown etched deep. A man ready to throw in the towel for the night. "Well? What is it?"

"A little backdoor cyber investigating," Devereux said. "Grab your coat. We're going to hack these bastards."

***

CHAPTER THIRTEEN

A LINE OF BALD MONKS in grey ceremonial robes leaned against the wall of a Zen temple, watching with spirited interest as a wave of drunk, half-naked women in pink stilettos strutted across the street. Above, as he slouched lazily against the rails of a construction rafter, an elder monk took a drag from his cigarette, cackling as the girls below shook their stuff.

The temple was the floor level of a rundown apartment building that was never finished. Beams of rusted rebar jutted off the sides of the structure as a crosshatching of rotten wood lay partially visible on the topmost floors. Portions of the building had been remodeled and refitted with Japanese columns and stone Shinto shrines. At the foot of the entrance, a stagnant, green-watered pond rippled gently as small beads of moisture fell from the sky. Beside the temple, a red wooden replica of a torii archway stood as the unofficial gateway into Little Tokyo.

Devereux saw Lily turn her head away as they walked past the gawking cue balls, knowing if she made eye contact, she'd be susceptible to a healthy dose of hisses and catcalls. Lily brushed her shoulder as they walked under the shadow of the arch. She was nervous. She had a right to be.

Beyond the archway lay the vacant remains of a small parking lot. A rusted chain link fence rattled as it swayed gently to a light gust of wind.

"How far is it?" Lily asked.

"Just around the bend," Devereux said pointing to a graffiti-marked wall. Devereux turned and saw the mural. He squeezed Lily's hand and sped for the corner. He had forgotten all about it. A warning. The mural was a painting of a samurai in a suit and tie. It wore a red, demon-styled mempo mask with a dramatically downward curving frown. The samurai held a katana to his side. In his other hand: the decapitated head of a ninja, his eyes staring lifelessly at the parking lot floor. Loud subtlety was the Yakuza way. The message was clear: *we own this town.*

"What's wrong?" Lily asked.

"Yakuza territory. Nothing that hasn't been dealt with before, but if they spot a lone police officer, well, they consider that a gift."

They turned the corner and it was all there. Little Tokyo, also known as J-Town. It consisted of five densely populated city blocks hosting bars, arcades, sushi joints, implant shops, and everything in between. And it was also under the shadowed control of the Yakuza syndicate.

Devereux nodded at Lily. "Welcome to the underworld."

Ahead, a torrent of lights and colors cascaded off blinking signs and onto the streets and walls beneath, bathing everything in its neon glow. A maze of clustered shops wound and twisted through the boulevards as leather-bound crowds swept through them like an army of frenzied fire ants. The sustained attack of Japanese synth music pounded and thumped against old, splintered doors scarred with the symbols of Nipponese scrawl. Above the neon jungle, towered the sleek, cube-shaped condos as they stood stacked atop one another, forming what was the illustrious housing sector of J-Town. The Japanese developers had long known that city ordinance had banned outward expansion. Up had been the only way left to build.

Up there, somewhere, were the hotels and fine restaurants. Up there, the Yakuza kept watch over their shadow empire below.

"It's all so beautiful," Lily said, stopping as she gawked at the electric carnival in front of her.

"Don't stop. Keep walking," he said as he pulled on her wrist. "Otherwise you might get bumped by a pickpocket."

"I don't have a wallet," she said, snapping her wrist away. She pulled her studded, black leather jacket in tight. She didn't like him touching her. He raised his hands in the air apologetically and shoved them in his coat.

"I'm sorry," he said. "I shouldn't have grabbed you like that."

Lily crossed her arms over her chest and broke two steps apart from his side. She was still in shock. He had no right to place a hand on her. He couldn't have even begun to fathom the trauma she sustained. Rape. Emotional, physical, mental. She'd been transformed into a living Bunraku doll. The limits to the horrors that men created were only bound by their imagination.

"It's okay she said," coldly. "Let's just get to where we need to."

He looked her over for the first time as she walked in the neon light. A black leather jacket hung a size too big around her torso. She wore blue jeans that squeezed her hips a little too tightly, outlining her curves as she walked. The biker boots were an interesting touch; apart from boosting her a few more inches off the ground, they added an extra edge of intimidation to her. Devereux wondered which previous scumbag owner sported the edgy duds. He decided he didn't want to know. But she blended in well just the same; shy of just a few piercings, she looked like a J-Town regular.

Devereux and lily walked towards the den of youth as the crowds shoved and shouldered clumsily up and down the block, effectively turning the streets into a conveyor belt of hedonism. Scores of kids in form-fitting leather jackets, skinny jeans, and geometrically tapered haircuts cruised the sidewalks while elder businessmen slumped against patio dining tables, sipping sake while receiving handjobs from high-priced escorts.

Lily got a taste of J-Town life right off the bat.

A man with a tussle of greasy hair wearing a tattered white tank top and pitch-black shades leaned against the door of a busy noodle house as the crowds snaked outside. He took a drag from his cigarette and exhaled a thick plume of smoke. "Organs, hearts, kidneys," he whispered staring at the ground, making sure to stay hushed below the electric drone of nearby conversations. No answer. After a moment, the man took one last drag and killed the cigarette. He draped a blood-stained apron over his head and entered the noodle house through the kitchen door.

Devereux and Lily walked past the restaurant; the smell of what might have been fried pork permeated the air.

"Why was that man whispering?" Lily asked.

"So he doesn't get caught. Not supposed to be running organs without Yakuza approval. Might be scamming, though. Lots of desperate people end up at County morgue with dog hearts sewed in their chests."

Lily winced. She tried to change the subject. "Why isn't Kinneman with us?"

"In case something happens. He's waiting in the car just outside the J-Town boundary. Until we know we have something, we're playing this one close to the chest."

"It's that bad over here?"

"Worse. I still don't feel comfortable bringing you along."

"I don't care. We need to do this."

Devereux scanned the crowds. A bald man stumbled out of a dingy, nameless shop and bumped into Lily. Several scars lined his scalp, where small patches of hair were starting to spring around like weeds through the cracks.

"I can hear colors," he shouted eyeing all the lampposts and neon signs. "I can actually hear them! It's so loud."

Lily stepped back. Panic in her eyes. The idea of strange men accosting her again struck a sour note. Devereux wrapped his fingers around the man's head and pushed. He stumbled backwards, falling on a puddle of grey water. The man shelled up in the fetal position and covered his eyes.

"Cyber drugs," Devereux said. "New wave of sensory stimulants. Must've gotten an implant in his head. Small biodegradable chips that fire off in your brain, causing a whole spectrum of sensations. When the chips burn out, they melt away. That's how they hook you. Soon, these guys have heads full of scars. No laws against them, though. Legislation's still pending."

Lily eyed the man with pity as she walked ahead. The

crowds stepped over his body as he shivered and rolled on the dirty puddle.

She looked away. "What are we looking for?" she said, impatiently. J-Town had already been too much for her.

"We're looking for RATs."

"Rats? How are those going to help us? Disgusting little things."

"Not rats. RATs. R-A-T. Remote Access Tool. Optical, sometimes neural implants that access networks and mainframes. Usually via a VR rig."

"No more implants, Detective," she said with a tinge of anger.

"No, not us. There's a group of kids running around the city. Mobile hackers for hire, really. They hit-and-run their targets for a price. They leech off wireless wavelengths and duplicate their ping, essentially creating a photocopy of the signal. Makes them virtually impossible to trace. Industrial espionage, keeping tabs for suspecting spouses, you name it, they do it."

"How come I've never heard of them on the news?"

"Because they're that good. Only one of them has officially ever been made. It's kind of an urban legend. Except they're very real."

"And where are they?"

"I think I'm looking at one now," he said nodding his head towards the side wall of a tattoo parlor. A row of bohemians lay sprawled against the wall in various stages of shooting up or passing out.

"Which one?" asked Lily. In the shadows, it was hard to tell them apart; their clothes were no more than grimy rags. She crinkled her nose. She wasn't sure if their stench had actually reached her, or if she had just imagined it.

"The one in the blue tattered rain jacket," he whispered. "The one shooting craps. He's got a hood over his head. Tell-tale sign."

Lily scoured the crowd. A pair of rag-mummies shot craps by the flicker of a dumpster fire; their shadows slouched over a perforated piece of cardboard. A man in a blue hooded jacket shook a tin can and fired off a pair of dice against the wall. The white cubes bounced off the cracking plaster, landing on a small puddle.

"Fuck," cried out a man in a tattered scarf. "No way. Not twice. That thing loaded?"

"Sorry, man, dice have no memory," the other man said. He swept his hand over a pile of credit cards and stashed his earnings inside his jacket. He twirled the dice in his hand and shoved them in his pocket. "Nice playing with you." He stood, lowered his head, and stepped out of the shadowed wall of the tattoo parlor and into the light of the street. As he walked, Devereux noticed the camo pants and military issue boots.

"He's leaving," she said.

"He's not going far."

The man walked across the street and sat half lotus style against the wall of a small teahouse. 'Free Wi-Fi' the crooked sign on the window read in static green letters. He lowered his head, the shade from his hood masking his face. He held out a gloved palm above his head as people walked by.

"He's just homeless," Lily said.

"It's a ruse," Devereux said. "Everybody knows you don't just whip out cash donations in a place like this. The smart ones ask for credit contributions. Get themselves a nice portable terminal, and ask for a generous swipe of the card. No, he's not homeless. Watch."

The hooded man crossed his arms around his chest. His head bobbed up and down out of sync to the beat of the music blasting on the street. His limbs started to fidget, as if trembling from the cold.

"Is he on drugs?" Lily asked.

"Not quite. From what I hear, it's a sensory experience, but he's not doing it to get high. I don't think. Follow my lead." Devereux crossed the street, making sure to time his footfalls with the rest of the crowd. As he neared the man, Devereux pretended to peer inside the shop windows, gazing at Lily's nervous reflections as she approached. He turned to her and put a finger against his lips. *Shh.*

The hooded man's head thrashed back and forth. His fingers curled in front of his face, like holding a marionette's crossbar. He flipped his hands over and closed them, pulling them in against his chest; an urban wizard in the act of casting a spell.

Devereux stepped toward the man. A woman in a bright purple kimono walked out of the teahouse and stepped between them. She bowed and gracefully motioned him inside the door with a sweep of her hand. Devereux scowled and shoved her aside. Too late. The RAT had already noticed him as he stood and pivoted toward the street. Devereux snatched the man's wrist, pulling away one of his gloves. A meshwork of circuits, cables, and rivets lined the man's exposed hand. The RAT snarled and broke for the heart of J-Town.

Devereux waved at Lily as he sprinted forward. He took in deep, controlled breaths as his feet pushed off the pavement. *Keep it steady.* He hadn't run in years; each lunge ached more than the last as his feet pounded against the cement, sending a bolt of pain vibrating through his bones. Devereux growled. His muscles knotted up, feeling like they were on fire now. The rush of wind against his face brought no relief as his lungs struggled for air.

The RAT cut a sharp corner, running into the maw of a dim-lit alley. Devereux ran in behind him. Lights flickered on and off as the electric buzz of false contact filled the air. Devereux felt a tight squeeze in his chest. *Ignore it, you're not gonna get a second chance.* He heard the loud steps of Lily's boots close behind. *Good, stay close.*

Devereux exited the alley.

The RAT was boxed in. The end of the alley opened up to a small, fenced-in turnaround. The alley led to the rear exit of a Japanese market. Two large dumpsters blocked the only doorway. A rusted chain-link fence stood between the man and his escape.

No way he'd climb it without Devereux reaching him first. Devereux clasped his chest, walked up slowly, and flashed his badge. "You nearly killed me. Next time don't run."

"Running's what keeps you alive around here," the man said.

"I don't want to hurt you," Devereux said huffing. "I'm just looking for someone that can help me. I'm looking for the Alchemist."

Lily caught up to Devereux. He waved her back.

"The Alchemist," he repeated. "Where is he?"

"Why do they call him the Alchemist?" Lily asked.

Devereux kept his eyes on the man. "Because he can turn plastic into paper, if you catch my drift."

The RAT flashed a mischievous smile. "You want help. And who's going to help me?" He removed his hood. A VR rig straddled his head like a helmet; one long, black curved lens wrapped around his face where his eyes would have been. His nose and mouth were exposed as he inhaled a deep breath.

"Alchemist?" Devereux asked.

The RAT nodded.

"I can help you. Tell me how."

"You're a cop?"

"Detective Audric Devereux. Vice."

The RAT flipped the obsidian-tinted visor behind his skull. The rest of the rig collapsed behind his neck as layers of metal and polymer shifted underneath themselves like thin tectonic plates. He was a young blonde man, mid-twenties. He looked clean-cut, with short, neatly trimmed sideburns and a buzz cut like a man who might've just enlisted in the army. Or run away from it. "Then there's zero chance you can help me."

"What are you talking about?" Devereux asked.

"An hour ago. I stole and transferred twelve million dollars from a secret Yakuza account."

"Why would you do that?"

"Not me. The guys who hired me. Wanted to drain their funds for when the time came."

"Who are your employers? When the time came for what?"

"Triads. And I don't know. A drawn-out war?"

"Are the Yakuza after you?"

"They will be soon. I entered through a LAN server. They know I'm close. I only stopped for a quick game of bones before I finished the transfer."

Lily nudged Devereux. "What's a LAN?"

"Local Area Network, if I'm not mistaken."

"Bingo. I had to physically break into a Yakuza terminal. Not fun. Don't like close-up jobs."

Footsteps. "Fuck," Devereux said. He turned to face the alleyway. In the flicker of fluorescent light two silhouettes approached cautiously, like predators stalking their prey. Devereux nudged Lily behind him.

The chain link fence rattled. Devereux turned again. Four hooded vagabonds spilled onto the dead-end alley, joining the cornered RAT.

The four quickly stripped off their hooded jackets and flipped their visors, their rigs compressing behind their heads. RATs. All of them teenagers. Three males and one female. They drew weapons.

The tallest one stood at about 6'5 with a grouping of studs and piercings covering his face. He was decked out in a sleeveless blue denim vest and heavy steel-toed boots. He squeezed the nail-studded baseball bat in his hands as he smiled.

A skinny Asian boy with spiked hair in a black and white Adidas tracksuit snapped his wrist and flicked a butterfly knife open. The small butcher shot an open hand forward as he pulled his knife hand back. He faced Devereux sideways in a crouched duelist's stance.

The third boy was also possibly the youngest. He lifted his oversized baseball jersey at the waist and whipped out a single, rusted sai from his belt. He twirled it in his fingers like a ninja.

The girl sported long brown dreadlocks with dark caramel skin to match. Her eyes were slightly Asiatic, hinting at her partial heritage. Besides Alchemist, she looked like the oldest of the four. She wore a faded blue t-shirt, black leggings and sneakers. A row of small hooped earrings sparkled like stars as they pierced both her ears. Her eyes glistened in anger as she stared Devereux up and down. She drew back her sleeve, revealing a wrist-mounted crossbow.

The scene looked like an old-school street fight and he had the luck of being at its center. "Your call, kid. Who am I shooting?" Devereux said looking at the RATs and back at the approaching silhouettes. He put a hand on his holster.

Two men who could've been twins stepped out of the shadows and directly underneath the orange light of a hanging lamppost. They were Japanese men in grey form-fitting suits with crimson ties. Their hair was just as slick as their duds. With gloved hands, they reached inside their jackets.

Devereux half-expected them to unsheathe their katanas and take up battle stances. Instead the man to his right retrieved an electric cattle prod from his waist. He squeezed his hand and small arcs of blue light sizzled up and down the baton. The man on the left reached inside his jacket and pulled out a compact, shotgun-like weapon with a thin barrel that tapered towards its end. He thumbed a switch and the gun started to whir loudly.

"Neural flechette," Devereux whispered to Lily, keeping his eyes on the Yakuza hitmen. "Don't let it hit you. It fires a buckshot of arrow tips carrying nanobots. If the shot penetrates your skin, the nanobots travel up your bloodstream and start eating away at your brains from the inside."

Lily pulled her jacket in tight, the only cover available.

"Help me get rid of them and I'll cut a deal," the Alchemist said, pulling a box cutter from his pocket.

"Deal," Devereux said as he unholstered his pistol. He pointed the weapon at the Yakuza hitmen in one hand and flashed his badge with the other. "Los Angeles Police Department. Throw down your weapons and place your hands on your head."

The men split apart, disregarding the command. Cattle Prod walked to Devereux's right side in a slow semi-circle stride, moving directly parallel to his shooting hand. Flechette moved to Devereux's left side, squaring up parallel to Lily. Devereux hesitated for a moment as he aimed the gun back and forth, finally setting his sights on the top of Flechette's head. He placed his left hand on Lily and guided her behind him, clearing his shot. Behind them, the RATs advanced forward. The five of them approached in a uniform line before fanning outward.

Flechette took a single step forward and raised his weapon. Devereux started to squeeze the trigger. A feint. Cattle Prod tossed his electric baton, striking Devereux's hand. The shock coursed up his arm, prying his grip loose. The pistol dropped.

Flechette took aim at Devereux's head.

A faint whir cut through the air as a rusty sai spun point-first into Flechette's trigger hand, knocking it off aim. The weapon discharged in a sharp motorized whine, sending buckshot colliding into the floor. The arrowheads ricocheted off the wet pavement, sending sparks flying from the ground as the nanobots short circuited on small puddles of water. By the time Flechette swung his weapon around for another shot, an arrow had already struck his right thigh. The Yakuza screamed, dropping his weapon. The big brute in piercings charged forward, swinging his nail-studded bat at the man's leg. The blow connected, driving the arrow deeper into the man's flesh. Flechette fell to his knees, howling in pain. The brute raised his bat behind his head for a finishing blow. Flechette spun his good leg, locking it behind his attacker's knee, sweeping the brute off his feet.

The brute hit the floor, the back of his skull connecting with the street. It sounded to Lily like the faint sound of a watermelon cracking. To her right, Cattle Prod dashed towards Devereux as he crawled on the street to retrieve his pistol. The Yakuza looked down and smiled. He kicked the baton, sending it flying back at Devereux's torso. An arc of electricity shot out of the contact point on Devereux's chest. He collapsed face first on the ground.

Lily lunged towards Devereux. Cattle Prod shoulder rolled forward, snatching the baton from the floor in a single fluid motion. He cocked his arm back; a strike meant for the back of Devereux's head. Lily shot an outstretched arm forward, intercepting the prod as it made contact on her synthetic skin.

The current coursed through her bionic arms and down her metallic spine, the shock locking her muscles in a grueling cramp. A sharp sting pierced deep behind her eyes. The blood in her head throbbed and pounded against her temples. With her free hand, she fought through the fire in her limbs and reached for the Yakuza's collar. She wrapped her fingers around his neck and squeezed, transferring the current through his body. The man's teeth clenched shut. Blood seeped out the gaps in his gums, spouting down his lips and chin. The baton fell from his hands. His eyes rolled back in his head as he passed out. Lily snarled. She wanted to squeeze until her fingertips touched again. She heard Devereux's moans and dropped the man.

Lily helped Devereux sit up. He appeared dazed, like a man waking from a drunken stupor. He tried to speak through labored breathing. "Muguh," he mumbled. He clutched at his chest. Electrical interference.

"I don't understand," she said.

He swallowed and took a breath. "My. Gun."

The scraping sound of metal dragging against rock made her turn. The last bloodied Yakuza picked up the nail-studded bat and hobbled to his feet. He plucked the sai from his hand and tossed it aside. The female RAT reloaded an arrow into her wrist chamber and took aim. She fired off a shot. The Yakuza flicked his wrist and swatted the bat, catching the arrow mid-flight. The wood splintered into small fragments, filling the air with dust. The boy in the Adidas track suit circled the Yakuza soldier, tossing his butterfly knife from hand to hand. Lily had seen men do this in the streets of Llagan.

The Yakuza's eyes darted left to right as the boy tossed the knife. The boy spit on the floor and flicked the knife from his left hand to his right as he placed one foot forward. In an act of perfect timing, the Yakuza swung the bat, knocking away the knife mid-trajectory. Using the momentum of the thrust to guide him, the man pivoted completely around and swung the bat, catching the boy in the right shoulder. A row of nails tore into nylon and skin. The boy dropped, screaming as he clutched his wound. The yakuza reached for the flechette gun.

Alchemist sprang and jumped, placing a well-aimed boot at the Yakuza's injured thigh. Blood gushed out, staining the man's sleek, grey suit.

"My gun," the voice came again, cutting into Lily's concentration. Devereux extended his hand, his fingers opening and closing. Lily snatched the gun off the floor and placed it in his palm, curling his fingers around the butt.

Lily turned again. Alchemist slyly palmed the box cutter as he walked behind the injured Yakuza. The man crawled on his hands and knees, reaching again for the bat. Alchemist flung the blade open and held the man's head back, exposing his bare throat.

The pain shot back in her head. Lily closed her eyes in anticipation of the oncoming bloodshed. She'd already seen too much of it. When would it end? She clasped her head with both hands and screamed, collapsing on the floor.

A loud gunshot cracked in the cramped air between the walls. She opened her eyes. Devereux stood over her as he aimed his pistol at the Alchemist, smoke billowing out the barrel. On the brick wall behind the RAT's head: a hole. A warning.

"Let him go," Devereux said, eyes scanning the rest of the RATs. Devereux turned to Lily. She shivered violently before blacking out on the wet floor. He turned to the kids, bloody and breathless. "Now, I'm gonna say it once, and once only." He lowered his pistol. "I need your help."

***

CHAPTER FOURTEEN

"SO LET ME GET this straight," Alchemist said stroking his chin in what Devereux perceived to be half interest and half concern. "You want me to hack into Paradigm Industries, the global fucking leader in military bio-tech? The corporation with one of the toughest firewalls in the world?"

Devereux looked at the sky. The clouds were disjointed and spreading thin like melting ice caps in a calm ocean. The storm had passed. Only the aura of the city and blackness above lingered overhead. Soon, that too would be washed away by the breaking light of the dawn. "I don't know how many times I have to tell you. There are very few people that have the resources to pull off this kind of procedure. Just look at all the pieces: the tech, the know-how, the funding. You know that's where you'd look first. What they did to Lily, what they've done to those four men- we have to stop it. Are you going to help me or not?" Devereux knelt beside Lily's unconscious body. He swept a strand of hair away from her face and cradled her head in his arms. "This girl is dying, and if you're not going to do anything, she won't be the last- "

"Whoah, whoah, whoah. I never said I wasn't going to help, Sleuth-Man. It's just that, this is something I- we've never done before." Alchemist turned to his crew. The big brute— Rigel Kent, Alchemist had said his name was— stared at them as he sat on a wooden crate against the wall, his body making a mockery of the small box. Beside him, the two unconscious bodies of the Yakuza twins lay on the floor, their wrists and ankles bound together by a pair of zip ties. With a quick scoff, Rigel returned his gaze to the project sitting on his lap. He jabbed a screwdriver into his VR rig and twisted; the fall had cracked a few screws loose. The back of his head was stained with dried blood as it was beginning to scab. A grid of old scars lined his head between multiple shunts where Devereux assumed the VR implants attached.

"If you can't help— "

"It's not that I can't. It's just that we haven't done anything this dangerous. Biggest thing we cracked was Seoul Central Bank for a rival of theirs. Mostly that was all Keyper, though. He was the best." He lowered his head.

Devereux let a moment pass by. "That's where I can help."

The female Alchemist— Syntax, she said her name was— spun her head, whipping her dreadlocks around her face like tendrils. "What do you mean?" Her eyes became thin slits, suspicious, angry.

"I don't have much," Devereux said. "But I do have something that might offer some peace of mind."

Kiko, the sai-twirling boy in an oversized baseball jersey took a cautious step toward Devereux. "*De que hablas?*"

His buddy, Joon, the tracksuit kid, leaned on Kiko's shoulder. His bandaged right arm hung limp at his side. "Yeah, what are you talking about?"

"I know about Keyper. I also know that he's awaiting trial on two separate cases. He was the ringleader, right?"

"He was like our father," Syntax said. "He took us in when no one else would. He's more than a ringleader. Talk."

"My last case. Two brothers running an online porn business, Smut Kings Productions. They were allegedly running a kiddie porn offshoot. Low-key stuff. Filming, distribution, all of it. It had first come to our attention via an anonymous email. The email listed their home address, phone number, everything. Sure enough, the email was spot-on. When we got there, we found rows of rusty cages along the wall. They had lined the insides with newspaper for the kids to sleep on while hidden webcams recorded the whole thing. Day and night. Worse than dogs. We found the brothers were taking in runaways, exploiting them for their audience. Long story short, we busted the whole operation.

Thing of it is, the Cyber Police weren't satisfied with the big catch. They wanted to know who had been streaming the show, including the person who sent the email. With Government help, they overturned our denials to grant them access to the department's terminals. They culled their resources and traced the source of the email back to a Mr. Henry Villanueva, also known as the Keyper, alleged founder of the RATs."

"If you knew him, you'd know he was trying to shut those guys down," Alchemist said, his hands balling into fists.

"He would never do anything like that for kicks. They got him all wrong," Joon said before wincing in pain from his shoulder injury.

Syntax walked up to Devereux. She jabbed a finger in his face. "If you were really working this case, and if you were a halfway decent detective, you'd know he was innocent."

"I do know," he said moving her finger away with the edge of his hand. "I know he only rode the stream so he could take those guys down. He assisted our investigation. The LAPD and the Cyber Police are currently collaborating on the case, sharing notes, evidence. CP wants to put him away for good. And this is where my offer comes in. If you help me, I'm going to testify against Keyper."

"What the fuck are you talking about?" Alchemist said, his hand hovering close to the blade in his right pocket. Rigel stood, his mass blotting out portions of the lamppost's orange light. Kiko went for his waistband.

"That Seoul Central Bank job. Once the Cyber Police raided his house, they confiscated his terminal, his VR rig. They linked that big number you guys pulled directly to him. And now he's facing extradition. My testimony is key. I was the lead investigator on the case. If I testify truthfully, he goes free, only to be shipped off to face South Korean Justice. You'll never see him again. They don't take too kindly to cybercrime."

Quiet.

The constant, static hum of the city came alive. Distant chatter, cars, honks, screams. Lily stirred. She opened her eyes. Two bloodshot orbs stared back.

"Hang in there," he said.

She took a hard swallow and nodded.

The RATs looked at each other in silence. Their eyes fell on Alchemist. A real stinger. A lose-lose situation. One of those losses came with a consolation prize.

"I lie and point the finger, say he was getting off on that stuff, he stays put in the California Penal System. You guys can visit. Ten years max; plenty of time to mount a defense against extradition. I say the truth, well, like I said— "

Syntax turned and walked away. She cupped her face in her hands. Alchemist paced back and forth, his boots crunching gravel and rotten stems of bok choy.

He let the offer settle in for a while. He turned to Lily. She slipped out of consciousness again. "So," Devereux said. "Are we doing this?"

Alchemist reached in his left pocket. He pulled out a pair of dice. He twirled them between his fingers and sighed.

"We roll the bones."

***

CHAPTER FIFTEEN

EAST 2ND STREET WAS a long one, even by L.A. standards. It cut across most of downtown and pierced through the heart of J-town like a yakitori skewer. It's also where the RATs decided to form their Jump Line.

The line began with Rigel on the corner of San Pedro Street and 2nd and ended with Syntax on the corner of South Central Avenue and 2nd. That particular stretch of block was the center of Little Tokyo. It consisted of a few cultural landmarks, the first of which was Japanese Village Plaza: a densely populated square lined with feudal era storefronts with tiled roofs and paper sliding doors where bonsai trees sprouted from concrete planters under the nourishment of neon lights. Here the locals and tourists bumped shoulders on the hunt for sake, sushi, bootleg vids, and *drogas*. The second landmark was the Community Center, where rustic museums and theaters sat like ancient custodians, watching their own erosion as chrome structures bullied their way upward and outward. The long strip of street ran through the very soul of J-Town and its ocean of wireless wavelengths, and it's where the RATs chose their entry point.

The job was a standard hit-and-run formation: every RAT stationed 200 feet apart from each other across the length of the block in a triangle formation. Rigel at the start of 2nd street with the odd numbered addresses, Joon across the street on the even numbered ones, Kiko across from him on the odds again and so on. In the event that one of them got crimped, any single RAT could replicate the previous member's last signal and leapfrog the information forward, creating a new opening and a relentless chain of precision cyber-attacks.

"Now, remember," Alchemist whispered, as he stared at the wave of approaching tourists decked out in sunglasses and 'I Love L.A.' caps. The engines roared as cars motored and weaved through cyclists and pedestrians crossing the street. "Paradigm isn't like the rest. They have those Cortech sentries patrolling their mainframe twenty-four seven. Those guys have direct access to their most sensitive files via brain shunts. They're basically human firewalls. Once you're in the upper echelons of the system, only certain brain patterns can activate the gates. Remember that, these firewalls are brain pattern entry only, so you'll need to let the brain scanner link up with you directly. Luckily for us the brain recognition software still runs on code, and if it runs on code, it can be fucked with. If the Cortechs spot you, they can tap into your neural line and temporarily freeze your brain until the Cyber Police show up." Alchemist looked around for any eavesdroppers. "You have your secondary targets pinned?"

Rigel nodded and smiled.

"Good luck." Alchemist walked to his spot down the street, blending in with the throng of tourists.

Rigel pulled his hood over his head and touched the back of his skull. The VR rig snapped forward, plates sliding over one another until the black visor clicked into place over his eyes. There came a slight whir as the Remote Access Tool booted.

He backed his spine against the wall of a small ramen restaurant. The sounds of ringing doorbells and sandaled feet shuffling in and out of the restaurant slithered inside his hood. He shook it off and tried to focus. His rig beeped. Big red letters splashed on his HUD: *Wireless signal (YokoYummy323) detected*. He nodded and let his rig latch onto the signal. His eyes motioned up and down the HUD, initializing the synchronization process. The small download indicator slowly filled a red bar on the bottom of his screen. A group of blonde tourists babbling in a Nordic tongue walked past him, their silhouettes like grey watercolor blotches on his visor. He fixed his gaze back on the HUD.

The download bar glowed and beeped. The YokoYummy323 ping finished the duplication process. He blinked and the world morphed in front of his eyes. The combination of VR tech and Keyper's clever programming had transformed wireless wavelengths into visual code. All information streamed invisibly; all the data flowing in and around everyone's head now had aesthetic form via computer graphic imaging. Streams of light shot out from every angle: up and down buildings; radiating from the pants of pedestrians; pulsing from speeding cars. The simulation was like the world had rebuilt itself on glowing waves of light. A crisscross of multicolored beams flew above his head— the Information Highway.

The first time Rigel ever experienced it, a vicious migraine buried itself in his head for about a week. He almost couldn't handle the sensory overload. Visual sonar was the best way to describe it. As a boy, he had read about bats bouncing off sound waves to form mental images of their surroundings. That was cool. This was cooler.

He raised a gloved hand; the sensors in his digits were primed. Rigel snapped his fingers and he became a dart of violet light. He was now the signal made manifest.

He shot upward and merged into a streaming river of blue data. Trillions of small particles filled the blue wave as it ripped forward at the speed of light. The stream reconstructed into a blue tunnel, like the ones downtown, complete with chipped walls, with graffiti scribble marking the spots where codes of virus still lingered in quarantine. In the real world, Rigel blinked inside his visor; in the digital, he morphed into a violet-tinted avatar of himself. He found it helped him navigate the stream as the mind had trouble adjusting to lightspeed travel. He blinked again and a slick, aerodynamic motorcycle popped into existence. Two thin tires sat underneath a forward-lurching frame. His avatar kicked a leg over the saddle. He flicked the ignition and the engine roared to life. It sounded like the droning of a generator and the thunderous roar of a lion. His foot kicked the gears into place and the tires spun against the blue floor, sending up a shower of sparks like a fiery pinwheel. He pulled the throttle and the bike shot forward like purple lightning.

Rigel had never dropped acid, but this is what it must have felt like; a torrent of colors whizzing by like some psycho roller-coaster in a laser-light show.

He exited the tunnel and the world opened up. Outside the blue road, the sky was infinite and black. Rigel could see the faint green and blue grids from the trails of other wireless signals crisscrossing through the city.

The outlines of buildings materialized and dispersed in an explosion of pixels as he zoomed by. A small group of riders sped next to him on the road, coming and going as they pleased. They couldn't see him like he could see them. They were YokoYummy323 patrons surfing the web as they waited on steaming bowls of salty noodles. He accelerated and the city flew by as thin needles of color stretched before him.

The VR rig was a unique piece of software/hardware. It processed and color-coded the different forms of wireless data around him. An invisible freeway system coursed through the city, and only a privileged few could see it. Encrypted wireless signals were coded to appear blue; those were like toll roads: you either paid up or asked somebody for their password. Green roads represented unencrypted streams; the public highways of the datumplane thanks to people who forgot to lock their Wi-Fi connection. Those colors represented the main highways, leading to anything and everything.

He blinked in Paradigm's web address. A smaller blue road telegraphed to his right side. He swung the handlebars right and shifted his body, sliding the motorcycle into a hard drift. Rigel corrected himself and exited the ramp.

A flash of brilliant light exploded as he entered the Paradigm website construct. Waves of alphanumeric, binary, and HTML code whooshed by, rearranging and reformatting into real-time images. Rigel smiled. He was in the virtual lobby of Paradigm's website.

The room was an expanse of white walls with a static, green floor, and a large pulsating sphere at its center.

He slowed the bike to a slow cruise, his tires rolling over a floor of glitching green binary code. Gyroscopic camera drones buzzed the room. They were the basic firewall programs, keeping an eye out for viruses, and spamware. Rigel dismounted the bike and walked toward the sphere. The transparent avatars of people accessing the website phased through his virtual body as they came and went.

The sphere had many facets like the body of a finely-crafted diamond, each a link to different door. Rigel touched a section on the sphere named Employee Login and phased through it.

He was in a dark, spacious chamber now. An in-between room. A sealed oval portal with a blue aura hovered in the dark. *Encrypted access. Please Enter Password.* The ghost coding of existing authorized passcodes flashed by in a jumbled sequence of symbols and numbers. They drifted in the dark, like books flying in the vacuum of space. Something caught his eye. A glowing group of symbols hovered toward the portal. Someone was logging in. He leapt and touched the password with an outstretched virtual hand, storing an exact duplicate of the coding before it phased through the portal. He nodded his head and the bike materialized again. Rigel backed up and swung the bike around so that he faced the portal directly. He lowered his head and gunned the throttle. The engine roared as he hit maximum velocity. The bike speared through the portal, shattering it into millions of flying blue fragments. *Access Granted*. He landed hard on the other side of the Employee Access Network.

He looked around. The world glitched and buzzed as images struggled to take shape. The floor became a broken green grid as an infinite number of concrete tunnels snaked along like a maze in a sewer. Rigel's rig was having trouble processing the Paradigm construct. The slam he took to the back of the head must have been messing with his peripherals. He was now viewing the world through damaged eyes. He shook it off. *Focus*. Rigel chose the nearest tunnel and accelerated. A mesh of thin copper wires ran along the walls of the tunnel, like the inside of a power cable. A loud crackle roared behind him. He turned to look. A wave of electricity swept in behind him like a tidal wave. He gripped the throttle and lurched forward, the momentum nearly wiping him off the bike. The sizzle of current neared his avatar as the blue light lit the sides of the tunnel. He lowered his head and flattened his back as the bike topped out at max speed. Up ahead, the tunnel ended and split left and right. A sharp sting burned his spine as the electricity crackled behind. His neural sensors had registered pain. Enough neural trauma could kill him. In the real world, Rigel grimaced. He clenched his teeth and balled his fingers into fists. In the virtual, Rigel cut a hard right. The wave of electricity surged left.

"Fuck," his shout echoed down the tunnel. Ahead, lights flickered violently like miniature pulsars. There were portals lining the side of the wall that read *Vacation Request Form*, *Memos*, and *Recycle Bin*. Not good enough. If this world was anything like the rest, the restricted files were most likely located somewhere higher on the construct.

He came to the end of the tunnel. At its end, one path plunged downward, the other, straight up. He chose up.

He whipped the bike onto the tunnel wall and ripped upward. The loud crackle of electricity boomed in the distance. The sound of sirens wailed throughout the construct. The Cortechs knew he was there.

He sped up the wall until the tunnel ended, spitting him out onto a flat, spacious mesa that overlooked the entire network. He stopped the bike at the floor's edge and looked down. From up here it all looked like a cybernetic Dali painting; the tunnels appeared like black tubes as they twisted and looped along the floor; portals hovered slightly off the ground like some mystic medieval chamber. Nothing made sense. Rigel smacked his rig. The digital construct fizzled and the image morphed. The Paradigm domain looked like a circuit board now, complete with giant capacitors and oscillators. Directly across the way, a single, flat platform spun counter-clockwise as it hovered in the air. It looked like a giant microchip. "I'm losing my fucking mind," he said aloud. No construct had ever been as surreal. Usually they resembled something out of a handheld console or retro arcade game. Virtual constructs had always been geometrical; straight lines; grids. Either his equipment was FUBAR, or the construct was consciously changing itself.

He stared at the floating platform; a glass sign hung above a single red portal. A pink neon light flickered inside the glass. *Restricted Access: Neural Login Required.*

Bingo.

Rigel exhaled and backed the bike up. He revved the engine and pulled the throttle. The bike thrust off the edge of the floor. He yanked the handlebars upward, whipping the bike into a jump. He landed on the platform and skidded into a hard brake. Too much momentum. He rolled off the bike in time as it slid off the edge. He watched the bike plummet into the abyss of the surrealist nightmare.

Rigel walked to the portal. A steel hose snaked from the other end of the door. It reached around the back of his head and probed his skull with a three-fingered clamp. It found Rigel's neural port and inserted a thin shunt. He blinked into his visor and activated the Overload Virus: a routine that generated an infinite number of clearance codes that overwhelmed the system's physical hard drive space, causing Random Access Memory to kick in in order to compensate. The virus then caused the RAM to become overwhelmed shortly thereafter, causing the system to thrash and collapse entirely. This was his only chance.

The virus activated and recoded itself by way of emulating Rigel's brain patterns. He felt numbness in his head for what seemed an eternity as the Paradigm software scanned his mind. He squeezed his eyelids shut; the real world was nothing but white noise now. Everything felt like a dream in a snowstorm.

He opened his eyes. The hose tore itself from his skull and lashed violently like a snake in its death throes. It retracted inside the portal as the red light turned green. Rigel jumped inside.

On the other end: the most beautiful nightmare construct Rigel had ever seen. A vast landscape of quicksilver labyrinths stretched for eternity. He was inside the topmost tier of

Paradigm Industries. On any other day, he would have found himself smiling. Today, he felt only fear.

Rigel entered the maze. The walls were running with melted chrome. His violet reflection contorted and dripped over and over again as he walked. In the far horizon, a faceted sphere spun on its axis in the air like a celestial body. A spinning conduit, it sent an arc of electricity plunging into the ground. The lightning branched outward, causing a terrible tremor in the ground. The blue bolts roared through the labyrinths as they approached. The Cortechs.

Rigel broke into a hard run. Every corner he turned led to a slew of new silver corridors. There were no signs of portals or trap doors or anything besides the expanse of twists and turns. The crack of lightning thundered nearer. *Fuck.* He turned a corner into a dead end. Rigel quickly backtracked. A new corridor appeared where it hadn't been before. A row of portals lined the metallic wall. Rigel sprinted for the nearest door. He tripped, his face slamming against the floor. A tsunami of electric current roared in from around the corner. Electricity bounced off the conductive walls, creating a larger avalanche of energy. He pushed himself off the floor and dove for the first door within reach. His body slammed into a solid structure. It was sealed. *Access Denied.* The system must've rebooted and flushed out the virus. He turned his head. The wave of lightning ripped through the tunnel, creating a blinding light in its path. It was going to hurt like hell. He grit his teeth. Before the wave consumed his body, he looked at the portal in front of him. Above the frame of the door, he read the words: Control Theory. He swallowed a hard gulp and all pain was manifest in a blinding white flash. Game over.

FROM THE STEPS OF a Japanese souvenir shop across the street, Joon watched Rigel spasm against the wall.

After a few moments, Rigel collapsed to the ground and lay motionless. The crowds walked around his unconscious body like it was spilled trash. Just another junkie strung out on some cheap synthetics.

Only a matter of time now before the Cyber Police showed up. Standard protocol. The Cortechs would alert the CPs to the approximate source of the signal and the witch hunt would commence. The CP mobilized within minutes, usually faster than the LAPD did. Data meant security; data meant money; and in this day and age those two things were the modern equivalent of salt and water in the ancient world.

The souvenir shop had a shoddy connection but it was enough to receive Rigel's last signal. Joon flipped his visor over his eyes. A purple string of light zapped directly into his rig and a bright, white tear in the fabric of reality opened in front of him. He pulled the tear apart with both hands and jumped inside. The rainbow of lights whizzed by him as he shot through the datumplane. Joon landed on a slowly spinning platform. A red portal stood before his purple avatar. He reached a hand out when a steel hose lashed at him like a whip. Joon rolled on his sliced shoulder, narrowly avoiding a sharp swipe. The pain registered in his neural banks; he cursed aloud on the steps of the shop as his howls echoed simultaneously across the expanse of the construct.

The portal was on alert; the firewall was now hostile to anything trying to enter. The Overload Virus Rigel had used to get inside the door was now, without a doubt, useless; the firewall would never fall for that trick again. Paradigm was officially a failure. He only had a brief window to hit his secondary targets before the CP arrived. Time to log out. He tucked his injured arm close to his torso and dove off the platform into the darkened depths of a nightmare construct below. A floor of twisting tunnels and razor-wire floors awaited as he fell. He blinked in a new set of coordinates into his visor and plunged into a new tear of white light.

Another blizzard of lights streaked past him as he rode the information highway. He fell into a new world and landed hard on his feet. The Dermalab website construct: the inside of a giant cube standing solely on the tip of one of its corners. The walls were divinely polished glass. Joon saw his avatar's purple reflection staring back as he marveled at one of Silicon Valley's gems. The space of the cube was filled with smaller cubes linked together by streams of electric current. Those had to be the company links and files, individually compartmentalized and sealed.

Sleekly designed elevators lined the walls around the cube, hoisting up the avatars of other users as they meandered to and from their destinations. Joon called one of the lifts and hitched a ride. A module on the inside of the elevator door asked him to enter his destination. He punched in *Shipping Records*. The elevator zipped upwards to the highest levels of the construct. The door opened in front of a crate-sized cube. "Please place hand on scanner," it said in a digitized voice. A touchscreen terminal appeared on the top of the cube. Joon planted a hand on the screen and activated the Friendly Fire Virus from his rig. The program was one of the first routines he had ever written without the assistance of Keyper. He was proud of not just its ingenuity but its effectiveness. It sought out the firewall program and renamed the file, causing the software to turn on itself, seeing as it appeared to be a foreign code. This left it scrambled and usually caused glitch openings all over the system.

A light scanned Joon's hand. The virus transferred flawlessly. The screen went black as it rebooted itself. A portal opened on the surface of the cube. Joon touched it and phased through.

He was now inside a spacious room filled with rows and rows of shelves with boxes containing manila folders. Their small tabs jutted out as the only indicator of reference. A glowing green sign above the room read, *Sort by: Date*. Joon frowned. The sleuth had neglected to say much in regards to specifics. It would be virtually impossible to sort through the files. He had an idea. Joon waved his hand. The folders flew through the room and rearranged themselves before settling in new locations. The sign above now read *Sort by: City*. Capital letters marked the individual rows now.

Joon approached the 'L' section. As he reached for the Los Angeles folder, something caught his attention in the real world. Two dark blotches hovered over Rigel's body. He flipped his visor back. Two asswipes in long brown coats prodded Rigel's body with shiny leather shoes. They always went undercover; it upped their odds of moving in on their targets. But it was them alright: Cyber Police, the Brown Shirts of the data world. Their eyes skimmed past the tourists and drunk locals, settling instead on every bohemian and vagabond slouched against a wall. Joon lowered his head and pulled on his jacket's drawstring, closing the hood tight around his head. He waited a moment before returning his gaze upwards. When he did, they were already looking at him. They started to cross the street. *Fuck.*

Joon stood and flipped his visor back down. He needed to retrieve any bit of information he could get. This wasn't for the sleuth. Not even for the girl. He felt bad for her, sure, but he didn't know her. Keyper he knew, though. Keyper was family. This run was for him. He turned and shuffled up the street. In the digital world, his avatar found the Los Angeles file and plucked it from the bin. Joon heard footsteps closing in. His avatar opened the file. It fizzled in a cascade of static, like a salt and pepper hurricane. The world went dark. The souvenir shop's signal had stretched thin before snapping off. He quickly perched his back against the wall of a dingy bar and turned his head. The CPs were closing in as they waded through smog-emitting cars and the orgy of civilians as they crossed the street. Joon waited on the bar's signal to load. When it did, the CP enforcers had already locked on his position. Their hands were reaching inside their coats. He hoped they were reaching for their badges.

Joon jumped on the bar's signal and teleported to his last location, stored via his VR rig's internal memory. He was there again, opening the folder. Scores of digital files packed tightly inside burst open in front of him.

He skimmed the documents. *Damn.* All clientele information was blotted out in streaks of black like classified CIA papers. No names, no addresses, not even the contents of the deliveries. Confidentiality was no joke in the biz. One thing stood out like a sore thumb. A pattern running on every single page. The stamp and seal of another company was listed on every delivery document. *SureShip Limited.*

Real world: the footfalls were getting faster and closer now, like rapid strokes on a keyboard. *Tap, tap, taptaptap.* No time. Joon beamed all the intel down the line and killed the connection. He flipped his visor. A stiff hand gripped his bloodied shoulder and pushed down. He hit the pavement. Joon rolled over onto his back. Two men in long brown coats and grey, pressed slacks stood over him. One was young, possibly a new recruit; twitchy, anxious, not very stable. The other was a veteran, with his silvered hair and perpetually-furrowed brow wrinkles. He looked like a mean son-of-a-bitch; the kind of guy who would turn in his mother for illegally streaming a movie. They wore sunglasses, masking their faces in anonymity. They were the anti-RATs; the boogeymen of law enforcement.

They whipped out their badges. The senior officer planted a shiny shoe on Joon's chest. "Face it boy, you've been crimped."

THE INTEL JOLTED KIKO'S rig like a bolt of lightning, almost knocking him down as he leaned against a wall; he could have sworn he felt the stream rattle his brain. He quickly filtered through the information as it zipped across the HUD. He pursed his lips and nodded as the files unfolded before his eyes. SureShip Limited. He'd never heard of it before. Time to get acquainted. His rig latched onto a massage parlor's signal as a suspicious geisha watched him from inside the window. After blowing her a kiss he took a step away from the parlor wall.

Before he punched in the SureShip web address, he saw Rigel stirring on the floor in the muck and litter. The big lug pushed himself off the pavement and dusted himself off. Kiko followed his gaze as it connected across the street. The two CP punks were shaking down Joon as he squirmed on the floor like a bug with its wings torn off. Kiko had known Rigel to be an intimidating guy, but a hothead he was not. Today was a different story. Kiko saw the blizzard of fury raging through his eyes as he flipped the visor behind his head. He could foresee the series of events unfold before they even happened, like some sort of prophecy: Rigel would charge the CP's in a maelstrom of fists and elbows, and he would fight gallantly as he did. The CP's would take a couple of licks, sure, but eventually they would back off a few paces, draw their guns, and pump him so full of lead, he'd be radiation proof.

    Kiko collapsed the rig behind his head and reached for his waistband. He twirled the sai in his hand and gauged the distance between him and the CP goons. They were both about 200 feet from Joon on the opposite side of the street. He could still beat Rigel to it if he hurried. He stuffed his hands in his pockets and briskly crossed the street. Rigel was pulling the hood off his head now as he started to cross, too. Kiko was 100 feet away now as he reached the sidewalk, narrowly avoiding getting hit by an illegally assembled dragster. Rigel picked up his pace as he stepped onto the curb and stripped off his jacket. The rig snapped behind his head as he flexed his large arms. He curled his fingers into balls of rocks.

    Kiko gritted his teeth and pulled the sai out of his pocket. He flung it at the window directly behind the CP's. *Crash.* They turned to him, stunned. He flashed them the bird and ran back toward the crowds. The CPs growled like wild dogs and sprinted after him. Kiko slid in between a pocket of drunkards, changing pace to match their steps. He turned. Rigel was already helping Joon to his feet. If they were smart, they'd be lost in the shadows in mere moments. Kiko flipped his visor over his eyes and tried to catch any connection he could.

    It'd be impossible to hold onto any signal on the move for long; eventually the connection snapped apart like an overextended rubber band. He had to stop somewhere. He weaved between a family of Mexican tourists crossing the street, the first time in years he'd been that close to a real family since his was gunned down in Michoacán. It all came flooding back. Cartel hit squad with the wrong address. Shot everyone as they slept. Immediate family, his cousins, all of them. They didn't know that he liked to sleep nestled between his parents, underneath the warm, woolen sheets. They hadn't seen him. Kiko Herrera mourned alone for days in the vermin-infested shack that was his home. Afterwards, he did the only thing he could do: he'd hacked the cartel's mainframe, discovered their ranch's coordinates, and emailed their address to their crosstown rivals. He left the country before the fireworks erupted.

He followed the family as they stopped outside a Japanese produce market to gloss over a large foldout map. He hovered close enough to blend in, feigning interest in the conversation. He lowered his head and checked for a connection. The market was running on a shitty, slow speed signal. No choice. He tapped in and nodded in SureShip's web address. There were footsteps all around him. *Focus*. His avatar zoomed through a storm of lights and phased into the SureShip website. Standard delivery company with a standard web construct. Cake. They were a carrier based out of Northern California that made frequent stops in Southern California. He sorted through the links and useless information littering its page. The login screen fizzled. *Come on.*

The family tucked the map away and started to move. Kiko accessed the SureShip login screen. Within 30 seconds, he had cracked it. He looked up. The family had cleared the street, leaving him exposed. The CPs locked in as they approached with their hands on their holsters. He took a step back. The men with guns were coming for him, this time under the banner of the law. He had never been caught, but immigrants had a nasty reputation for winding up dead around these parts. A churning sensation erupted in his stomach. He wondered then, how his family must've felt as the lead kissed their bones.

In a blurry streak, something bulldozed through the CPs, knocking their bodies over like bowling pins. Alchemist stood over the Cyber Police. He gave Kiko a wink. "Tag me, kid," he said.

Kiko shot him the information. Alchemist gave him a thumbs up as he sprinted up the street.

As Alchemist ran, the first slivers of light broke on the horizon. Soon, the shadows would crawl away to die. The streets were emptying out now as most shops had begun closing their doors. Nowhere left to hide, not as many connections to ride.

Time to hurry.

THE INFORMATION BUZZED ALCHEMIST'S visor. He swerved through a smattering of tourists and transients as he tried to process the information. Paradigm had been a fail. Dermalab was a no-go, too, except for the SureShip connection. They were a shipping company based in Silicon Valley. He juggled scanning through hundreds of files and addresses while simultaneously avoiding tripping on the cracked sidewalks.

He found something. Dermalab was a specific market. Too specific for anybody to be placing orders on a whim without proper reason or financial backing. There were two major Los Angeles routes; both whose shipments originated at the Dermalab address. *Check*. There was something else. The first address was blacked out. Restricted info. No time to crack it with the CPs hot on his ass. The second was a residential listing in Highland Park, a run-down community in Northeast Los Angeles. He'd rarely gone there himself. The connections there were trash and the gang violence there rarely made jobs worthwhile.

Interesting. Not much but it was something. He had to make it count. The Sleuth-Man had said he needed whatever they could dig up to be admissible. That was just code for 'make it public'. Alchemist smiled. He liked the sleuth's style.

As he ran, a sharp burst in his right leg, like a bolt of hot pressure digging through his flesh. The crack of thunder followed soon after. He took another step, and his leg gave out, wobbling like a steamed noodle. His face ate wet sidewalk. An almond-sized exit wound gaped through his right thigh, pulsing blood rhythmically onto the street. His hands gripped the floor and he pulled himself forward. Footsteps approached. He rolled over on his side and looked behind him. Smoke was billowing from the barrel of the senior CPs sidearm. *Goddamnit*.

The younger officer drew his weapon and broke from his partner, circling to face Alchemist's torso. The senior CP stayed put, keeping his pistol trained on his head.

"Don't fucking move, you cybertrash piece of shit," the young CP said, clicking the hammer of his pistol back.

"Keep it down or the Yakuza'll get you," Alchemist said.

A cool breeze sifted in, bringing with it the smell of rotting fish and vomit, the aromas of end-of-night in J-Town. On cue, the first golden rays of the sun lit the morning sky. That's when RATs were supposed to turn tail and scatter into the alleyways that spat them out.

Alchemist turned his attention away from the rot in the air and the pain in his leg back to his visor. He brought his gloved hands up slowly, sifting through the waves and signals of the datumplane.

"I said, don't move!"

The words sounded distant like the faraway sounds of ocean waves crashing against rocks. He nodded, but not at the officer. His hands weaved a spell as his virus procured him entrance through exclusive gateways like some sacred cyber Valhalla. He was inside SureShip's website, playing God as he tampered and tinkered, merging their private shipping files onto a brand new public link he named simply, *Routes*. Now anyone could see SureShip Limited's routes and addresses on a whim, if they were into that sort of thing. Say, even a judge itching to sign off on a warrant to track down a killer of suits and women.

"He's hacking something, kid. Don't let him finish," the sound of a hoarse, old voice shouted behind him somewhere.

"Don't fucking move or I'll blast you. Final warning," the CP kid said.

Through the smoky tint in his visor, Alchemist locked his sights on a woman decked out in piercings and dreads as she walked past him with her hands buried in her jacket. She pulled a hood over her head and winked at him. She was gorgeous. In another life, she could've been a great lover. In another life, maybe he'd finally have the balls to ask her out. He nodded her way, smiled, and with his thumb and index finger, shot her an imaginary round.

A blast reverberated through 2nd street. Alchemist's head jerked back violently as metal screws and grey matter sprayed the air.

A different kind of jolt struck her, too. The information

punched her head and streamed before her eyes. The end of the job. As Syntax walked she lowered her head and fought the urge to scream and cry. That, in itself, was the hardest job she ever had to pull.

And as the sound of sirens approached in the distance, she found all she could do was simply keep walking.

KINNEMAN HAD ALREADY FALLEN asleep at the driver's seat. Devereux envied him. How long had it been since he'd slept? He shook the thought and rubbed his eyes. Something moved in his peripheral vision. He looked out the window. Syntax's steps made no sound as she approached the car like a widow at a funeral, hands buried in her pockets and shoulders slumped forward. She placed her hands on the passenger side window and drew a deep breath of smoggy morning air. Devereux had heard the shots popping on the other side of the block as the sirens came soon after. The rest of the RATs had already scuttled out of the alleys like their namesake animal counterparts as they waited nervously for the rest of the team to assemble. One by one they hobbled in, battered and breathless. They kept their distance from the car, unsure if it was all really one big sting.

Syntax shot the backseat a glance. Lily was asleep, sprawled out, legs pressed against the door. The RAT looked back at Devereux. She swept a tendril of dreadlock away from her face.

"It's done."

"Alchemist?"

"He's mush," she said looking at the floor.

Devereux pursed his lips and reached for her hand. She pulled away.

"Don't," she said straightening up, regaining some of the fire he'd seen in her eyes before. "We pulled a single address from a shipping company called SureShip Limited. They make deliveries for Dermalab across the state. There was another address but we couldn't break it in time. The one we did get is a location in Highland Park. It's all public now. Check their website."

"And Paradigm?"

She raised an eyebrow. "Like we told you. No one can crack that place. Before Rigel got fried on his Paradigm run, he uncovered a top-secret file named Control Theory. The file was inaccessible even from the inside. Layers upon layers of firewall in that place."

"Control Theory?"

"Yep."

"Right. Thank you. Listen, Syntax, I'm going to honor our agreement. The trial's not slated for another couple of months, but when I get called in— "

"Yeah, yeah. I'm not worried about your word, Sleuth-Man. We know how to get to you either way. I have a bigger problem on my hands right now." Syntax turned to look behind her. Three young men, kids basically, hugged a brick wall as the last of the shadows dispersed behind the dumpsters and nooks that spat them out. They were whispering among themselves, confused. They were waiting on someone who'd never show.

Devereux looked at them and thought about Robert. Young, lost, ready to break. "I know what it's like," Devereux said. She turned to face him again. "Broken family, unsure of the future, no one there to help, I know. Bit of advice. You don't have to be a mother to them. Too much pressure."

Syntax lifted her hands off the window and took a step back. "No? Then what should I have to be?"

"Just be in their lives. That's it. There's a youth home on Fourth Street- "

"We don't need a youth home," she said defensively.

Devereux nodded and plucked a business card from his coat. "Take this. It's my card. If you ever need anything, you won't have to hack anything to get to me. Just pick up a phone."

Syntax took the card hesitantly from his hand and shoved it in her pocket. She turned and started walking towards the kids. "I hope you find whoever you're looking for," she said.

"Me too," he said under his breath. He turned to Kinneman. "Wake up. It's about to get hot."

***

CHAPTER SIXTEEN

THEY DARTED THROUGH MORNING traffic as they scrambled toward the station, avoiding the usual traffic accidents and never-ending construction zones. Everything was there on the website, just like Syntax had promised. A single Los Angeles address listed as a recipient of Dermalab's shipments. The shipments had been steady over the course of several months. They'd hurried to convince the District Attorney before SureShip noticed any glitches in their website. They'd made their case that it was too strange a fact that a residential address in a rundown neighborhood would be receiving very particular and costly items. Items found surgically implanted in Ms. Lily Santos.

The D.A. had a judge sign off on it in a heartbeat. Kinneman joined Devereux as joint lead on the raid. They'd been asked if they wanted to hand over duties and get some rest. Devereux wasn't sure if it was sleep deprivation or the elation of the end being in sight, but he couldn't remember the last time he laughed so hard. He would see the whole thing through. For Lily and Alchemist. For all the other unknown victims.

He poured over the facts as Kinneman briefed the Tactical Entry Team. The address in Highland Park belonged to Marcellus Fontaine. Devereux familiarized himself with the files as he flipped through the dossier. *Know the facts, know the man.*

Marcellus Fontaine was many things. For starters, he was vermin. He was an ex-con and a known political rouser. If anyone could summon the spark of social unrest and hellfire, he was the man. Devereux had seen men like him on the news time after time. Angry men who barked behind podiums, who slammed their fists and cursed the world as they promised vague answers and bold actions. Rabble-rousers was the term he remembered his father using to paint the men that had led the world astray.

Fontaine. Caucasian, sixty-nine years old. The man had gotten his start as an ER surgeon in San Francisco before moving to Los Angeles where he undoubtedly received a considerable bump in patients with bullet holes in them. He did it for years; countless overnight shifts receiving scores of L.A.'s dead and dying. Then one day he'd packed it up and retired. He'd stopped showing up to work. His colleagues just assumed the L.A. violence was too much; he'd picked up his golf clubs and headed to greener pastures.

A few years later he reappeared.

Fontaine came back a Transhumanist; a member of an intellectual movement that sought to 'enhance' mankind through the use of genetic, prosthetic, and cognitive modifications. The movement believed that the next step in evolution was a merging of biology and technology as a natural course of the human time-line. Fontaine had published several op-ed pieces in some underground tech magazines and had even managed to circulate some cheap pamphlets throughout his inner circle.

He even funded a black-market clinic that conducted illegal operations on affluent clients. Procedures that included experimental plastic surgery and prosthetic alterations. The city caught on and shut the whole thing down. He did time in State prison before being released early for good behavior.

Eventually he formed a sizable following that campaigned for legislation that would legalize medical and cosmetic prosthetic surgeries. The group called themselves The Neo-Gen Movement. When Neo-Gen didn't get their way, they were known to stir civil unrest wherever they went. Like over twenty years ago when they started a full-blown riot outside the steps of City Hall. Innocent bystanders were caught in the maelstrom of Molotov cocktails and mob violence. When the smoke cleared, fifteen, including two police officers, were among the dead. Fontaine was charged with inciting a fatal riot and did fifteen years' hard time. When his time was up, he faded back into obscurity. Until now.

Which brought Devereux to the present: somewhere along the way Fontaine went from patching people up to molding them in his own perverted image. Devereux wondered how a man could just switch gears, from mending people to murdering them. The why didn't matter at the moment, he supposed; they could always learn that later, if at all. Stopping him was what mattered. But his politics, his entire agenda was a big, red, bloody flag. Paired with the revelation of his discreet synthetic skin shipments, his whole rap sheet made him a chief suspect.

It was a warm morning. The rain had dried up, evaporating into a thin layer of smog that hung in the air like a toxic blanket, coating everything in a haze of grey. The sunlight lit the city, exposing all of its ugly little details. All the imperfections of Los Angeles were in plain sight: graffiti, vegetation overgrowth, pot-holes. The city, like a whore, looked better dressed at night.

Devereux and Kinneman drove point with the rest of the interceptors blaring their sirens close behind. Kinneman drove the cruiser like a race car driver, barreling down straightaways and cutting sharp corners. The engine roared like angry thunder.

Devereux turned to the backseat. Lily grimaced as she rubbed her temples. She had been fighting off a recent bout of migraines. They had gotten steadily worse over the last hour. He shot her a smile that went unnoticed. She hadn't recovered her memory yet, but she insisted on coming along for the ride. From a safe distance the sight of the suspect might spark something, she'd argued, and she could possibly make a positive I.D. on him. They had nothing to lose. They'd already gone through so much; she was basically a partner at this point. The department had no objections to her presence as an 'advisor'. His only demand was that she stay in the car with an armed escort. She had agreed.

Devereux placed the dossier on his lap and went over the file again. Fontaine's current address was listed as 1139 on Avenue 53, a back house in Highland Park, a small community with a split personality. Equally grimy as it was pretentious, it was home to numerous working class Hispanics, street gangs, and white hipsters who wielded the weapons of gentrification.

The car cut into a narrow street. Overgrown weeds served as motes to run-down homes while discarded dolls kept silent watch on littered sidewalks. They pulled up to a dry, golden lawn with patches of dead grass and shriveled horseweed. Five other interceptors fenced the lead car, creating a small circular perimeter, blocking the rest of the street from curious pedestrians.

The front house stood tall and ancient; it was one of those hundred-year-old homes that sprang from Los Angeles like a cracked tombstone in a graveyard of chrome.

Two chained Rottweilers greeted the policemen with growls before their owner reeled them in. The team leader, Lieutenant Cornell, motioned the man inside.

Devereux drew his sidearm.

Kinneman pounded Devereux's chest and flashed a smile.

The entry team shimmied past the narrow walkway between the wall of the front house and the rusted chain link fence that separated the neighbor's yard. Termite holes too deep to fix speckled the house's flaking walls. The house, Devereux thought, was like a metaphor for the old Los Angeles he'd heard about; what was once beautiful and elegant was now on its last legs and ready to topple.

The backhouse was a small unit, built illegally ages ago. Like the front house, it was in disarray with its small dilapidated windows and a discolored door. Small chips of paint collected like fragments of dry leaves underneath. An old bicycle from the previous century lay discarded on the driveway.

The officers took their positions by the wall alongside the door. He'd never actually participated in a raid; he'd always coordinated them from the safety of a tactical van or unmarked car in the sidelines. There were seven officers including Kinneman and himself. A handful of men stayed by the car with Lily.

The tactical vest squeezed his torso. He took a breath as deep as the gear would let his chest expand. The vest was composed of a special ballistic weave that stopped small-arms gunfire as well as knife thrusts. He exhaled and brought his pistol to his sternum.

Kinneman knocked on the door, "Marcellus Fontaine, this is Detective Kinneman of the Los Angeles Police Department. We have a warrant for your arrest. Please open the door."

No answer.

Kinneman swiped his digital card through the reader on the door. All homes were mandatorily retrofitted with card readers for purposes of home identification and police procedural matters. Amidst the war, the government did away with specific privacy rights as crime surged through the nation. This facilitated police matters with criminal arrests and the detention of Red Crescent sympathizers.

The warrant processed as a little light blinked green. The door automatically opened.

Lieutenant Cornell took lead and charged in, shotgun-first. A line of policemen followed immediately behind, like a well-orchestrated ballet. Devereux went in last, just behind Kinneman.

The house stank of rot: rotten food, rotten trash, rotten books. Devereux shook it off and tried to focus. The room was dark inside and his eyes were having trouble adjusting. The team switched on their gun-mounted flashlights and swept the room with thin beams of light. The only windows were boarded up with planks of broken tables. The only source of light was the sunlight at their backs. After a brief moment, his eyes adjusted enough to see the mess sprawled across the living room. Towers of moldy books sprang up from every nook, oftentimes spilling over as if regurgitated by some unseen monster. Piles of old hard drives littered the floor like discarded children's toys. Lieutenant Cornell waved the all-clear.

The hallway that connected the living room to the kitchen was a narrow walkway. Devereux's elbows touched the walls as he drew in his sidearm closer against his chest.

The hallway opened to a small kitchen, where cockroaches scuttled through a stack of unwashed plates, their black, shimmering shells hovering over old, caked-on stains. Devereux gagged and fought the urge to throw up. He looked away. *Keep moving.*

The team approached the back end of the building. The property housed an even smaller house than he imagined. Just now Devereux could see the last two rooms up ahead as he exited the kitchen. Lieutenant Cornell kicked in the first door to his right. Nothing but an empty bathroom that stank worse than the kitchen.

Cornell gave the all-clear again and moved into position outside the last door; he nodded to his second-in-command, Sergeant Flores, who lifted his leg and kicked the door down, sending a storm of bolts and splinters into the air. The line of officers streamed in like fire ants. The bedroom was empty save for a single piss-stained mattress. The men cleared the corners and checked under the mattress. No one.

In the back, Devereux saw something. A single door against the back wall. He motioned to Cornell with his thumb. Cornell turned the knob. The backyard was a small patch of dirt and dried grass and not much else. Something else. An old, unlocked cellar door along the back wall of the house. Cornell opened it. A narrow staircase led down into a well-lit basement.

The entry team started down a path of cracked concrete steps. The faint hum of electricity filled the room. Devereux felt beads of sweat drip down his ribs. He wondered if it was the heat, or nerves, his body's reaction to the terror that preceded the truth.

At the bottom of the stairs, fluorescent lights lined the ceiling of a spacious cellar, possibly the converted remnant of an old war bunker. A variety of old machines lined the concrete walls: computer monitors, generators, arc welding tools. One, an antique icebox from the 1950's, gave Devereux the impression that he didn't want to be the first to open it. Ahead, in the center of the room, a naked, limbless woman lay motionless on an elevated surgical table.

The scene was something out of a horror film he'd seen once. Mad scientists, evil experiments and all. Devereux felt a tickle along the back of his neck as small hairs started to rustle.

Sergeant Flores lowered his weapon and approached the woman as the team stayed locked in a covering position. He placed his index and middle finger along the side of her throat. "She's alive," he said.

From behind the shadow of a generator, a man lunged at Flores, plunging a scalpel into the side of his neck. A thin geyser of blood erupted from Flores's throat, spraying the woman and attacker simultaneously. Flores dropped.

A loud burst of gunfire filled the tight confines of the room. A sharp pain shot through Devereux's ears like a shank thrust. In a matter of what must have been two seconds, the fire ceased. Beneath the table laid the bleeding bodies of Sergeant Flores and his attacker.

Cornell moved in on the attacker, digging a knee into his back and handcuffing him. The man spat out a wad of blood, most of it splashing on his own beard. One of the officers gently lifted Flores's wrist and checked for a pulse.

"He's not breathing, sir," he said turning to Cornell.

"Fuck! Radio for a medic. How's the girl?" he said turning to Devereux.

Devereux approached the woman. She was completely naked save for a small oxygen mask strapped to her face. She was unconscious, her small breaths filling the mask with small beads of moisture.

"She looks like she's been anesthetized," Devereux said. He removed the mask from her face. "We need those medics in here quickly."

The officer turned away and spoke into his shoulder-mounted radio.

"Is this him? Is this Fontaine?" Cornell asked digging his knee deeper into the man's back. The man's muffled moans bounced off the floor.

Kinneman crouched beside the man's squirming body. "Looks like him. Dev?"

Devereux studied the man's face. He'd remembered the defining features from the old photographs: thin lips, pointed chin. All his features were now obscured now by the long, white beard of an old man.

"Hard to say," Devereux said. "There haven't been any recent photographs of Fontaine. He went recluse after he served his sentence." Devereux pulled a folded picture of Fontaine from his pocket and held it up to the dying man. The man pinned on the floor had the same blue eyes and the same thick brows. "Yeah, looks like him."

"Marcellus Fontaine," Cornell growled. "You are under arrest for multiple counts of murder and kidnapping."

The man on the floor smiled. The grin of a lunatic. His clothes were soaking up the expanding pool of blood under his body. "I didn't kidnap anybody," the old man gasped, his breath spraying up blood off the floor.

"Bullshit," Kinneman said. "We caught you red-handed. Open and shut case if I've ever seen one."

"I don't know what you're talking about." His lips formed small rings as he struggled to take in a breath like a fish gasping for water.

"The girls," Devereux said. "We know you've been kidnapping women, practicing illegal medical procedures on them. You've been turning them loose on Paradigm executives."

Fontaine laughed in a staccato burst, stopping every few seconds to catch his breath. Devereux guessed collapsed lung from the gunfire.

"Wrong," was all Fontaine managed to say.

"Wrong?" Kinneman replied. "What about that poor girl right there?" he said pointing to the unconscious woman.

"You've been buying large shipments of collagen polymers," Devereux added. "The best fake skin money can buy. Very expensive for an old man living in a shit shack in Highland Park. Tell us where the other girls are, before it's too late."

Fontaine licked his bloodied lips. "That woman is a client. I perform on amputees. Give them prosthetics. It's all under the table. Haven't killed anyone."

"Not directly, no," Devereux said. "We know about the mind control implants."

Fontaine shook his head. Genuine confusion.

"You're a Transhumanist. You believe that everyone should undergo these procedures, right? That it's the next step in evolution? You've been kidnapping girls off the streets, mutilating their bodies, and using them to murder prominent businessmen. Fancy Transhumanist science there. Maybe old clients? Unpaid debts?"

"Detective," he said, gasping for a long breath. "We believe in the improvement of the human body through technology in order to eliminate congenital mental and physical barriers." He shut his eyes, every word that came out of him looked like it hurt. He opened his eyes with a youthful fire in them. "In order to achieve the post human stage of existence, we believe in a course in which individuals forsake natural evolution for a deliberate one; it is in a way its own natural selection." He paused to draw another breath, blood spewing from his mouth like lava. "I couldn't give two fucks about those girls. I wouldn't perform any procedures on anyone that couldn't afford them." Fontaine narrowed his eyes, fixing them on Devereux's. "Time weeds out those unworthy of Transhuman evolution. Those who adapt to the change will be stronger for it. Those who can't afford the means to undergo the knife will be scraped off the genetic timeline. Even if I could afford to perform these procedures, I wouldn't bestow it upon some nameless slut."

"Lieutenant," Devereux said. "Have the men bring Ms. Santos in here so she can identify the suspect."

Cornell spoke into his radio as he took the knee off Fontaine's back. The rest of the entry team had secured the nooks behind every table and generator in the room. All-clear.

Devereux looked around. A pair of prosthetic arms lay on a small table beside the naked woman. Thin wires jutted out the ends of the artificial limbs. The arms were ready for soldering onto the woman's nerve endings. Fontaine was about to begin the operation when they had arrived.

Lily was escorted into the cellar. A crew of medics came in behind her and lifted Flores off the floor and loaded him onto a gurney. They rushed him out of the room with the urgency of wartime surgeons.

Another EMT knelt beside Fontaine. Kinneman waved him back. "Lily, I want you to look at this man. Is there anything you remember about him?"

Cornell yanked Fontaine's collar, pulling him up onto his knees. His head struggled to stay upright as his life slowly slipped away. He wore green surgical scrubs, now riddled with acorn-sized entry wounds and large blotches of blood.

Lily looked at Fontaine and back at Devereux. She winced. Devereux saw the horror in her eyes. Staring at mortal wounds was never easy, he knew.

"It's alright," Devereux said. "Just take a look and we'll wheel him off to the nearest hospital."

Lily stood there in the same clothes as the night before except they were wrinkled now, and her hair was a wiry mess. She had managed a few moments of sleep but it hadn't eased the pain. She looked at Fontaine. Her eyes studied his face. Without a word, she stepped away from the man and walked around the room. She looked at the walls, the floor, every apparatus and electrical device. She approached the unconscious woman and cautiously extended a hand. Lily's fingers made contact with the woman's skin. She gently caressed her forehead. Tears welled in Lily's eyes.

Devereux could only imagine the trauma ripping at her insides.

Lily broke contact with the woman and walked back to Devereux.

"It's not him," she said.

"What?" Kinneman said, half shocked, half outraged.

"I don't remember this man. Or this place. I've never been here. I remember rusted walls. I was inside a large room. And it was dark."

"There's gotta be some kind of mistake," Kinneman said. "Look at what he was about to do to this woman."

"I know," Lily said wiping the moisture from her face with the back of her hand, "but as I was walking here I remembered something. The man who kidnapped me..." She fought hard not to cry again as her eyes began to well again. "That man drove a dented white van."

It hit Devereux in the gut. The driveway. An old bicycle. Fontaine's file had made no mention of having a vehicle registered under his name.

A loud gasp. Fontaine wheezed as he struggled to draw air into his porous lungs. He convulsed for a violent fraction of a second before his limbs went limp. Cornell dropped Fontaine's dead body onto a pool of his own blood. Fontaine's face smeared a broad crimson streak across the floor like the stroke of a paintbrush.

Devereux felt his eyes getting heavier. He hadn't slept in so long. How long now? He didn't know. The world seemed like a blur. He holstered his pistol. Out there, a killer still roamed free.

He stared at Fontaine's lifeless body as it basted in its own juices. Eternal peace. The long sleep.

And as he looked down on Fontaine, for a brief moment, Devereux felt only envy.

***

CHAPTER SEVENTEEN

THE MIDDAY HEAT SWELTERED as the sun's light pierced through Devereux's office window. Outside, waves of hot air surged across the horizon like a mangled mirage as summer's stranglehold on early autumn continued. The cars on the street below pumped stacks of black emissions into the sky like the dirty plumes of oil drum fires. Devereux shut the blinds and loosened his tie. The room became dark but trickles of sweat still streamed down his cheek like warm teardrops. He cursed the broken air conditioner under his breath in broken French.

Kinneman had called it a day and decided to head home. He was lucky. Devereux's shift had been even longer. His terminal stated the date: Saturday, September 27, noon. He'd started his shift at 6 AM, Friday morning, doing file work on a previous case. What had dropped on his plate had shattered the mundane pencil-pushing routine of police work. Mind control? Cybernetics? Mutilations? Kidnapping? Perhaps that was a little too much for L.A.'s Vice department. And it had been costly. In just a few hours the tally had been colossal. Where did it end?

Four people murdered; a dying, mind-controlled killer cyborg; a splattered hacker; a mortally-wounded police officer; and a bullet-riddled false lead later, and he was nowhere closer to finding his killer. The department had since scrambled to invest more resources on the case. As for him, his shift was over. They'd told him to finish his report, go home, and get caught up on rest; Vice was being taken off the case, the guys in Homicide would take it from here.

He stared at the report on the terminal screen. It all looked like one big run-on sentence blasted with typos. The longer he stared at the screen the heavier his eyes felt. He shook it off. This case was too screwy. Was it all a dream? Some hyper-hallucination of his mind's working?

The door to his office opened. Lily walked inside. An all-too-real look painted her face. A look of hurt that couldn't be dreamt. No, all of this wasn't a dream. The human mind couldn't comprehend certain things, and substituted easier explanations in their stead. In this case, he had just wished it was a dream.

"How are you, Detective?"

"Just call me Audric," he said as he put his hand on his forehead. It might've been his body shutting down on itself or perhaps the sympathy pains associated with Lily, but he felt the onset of a wicked headache lurking. "Would you like to sit down?" He motioned her towards the couch in the office.

She shook her head. She was still untrusting of him. He couldn't blame her. He wasn't an expert but he had to take into consideration that she might be suffering from Post-Traumatic Stress Disorder.

"Alright, well, I'm gonna sit." Devereux walked toward the back of the office and sank into the couch, letting his legs spread out. He tilted his head back and closed his eyes.

"I'm sorry," Lily said.

He looked at her. Her hands were clasped together in front of her like a child at the principal's office. She felt guilty.

"You have nothing to be sorry about."

"I'm sorry that man wasn't who we were looking for. I wish my memory was back. I wish I could tell you more, but I just don't remember."

"It's not uncommon to have amnesia after traumatic events." Devereux looked at the Venetian blinds. A narrow beam of sunlight pierced underneath a single broken slat through the window. "That's us, Lily. A ray of light in a dark room. We do what we can, right?"

"My mother used to say something like that. She would say, 'even in the certainty of darkness, you should always be your own light.'"

"Wise woman. Have you contacted her yet? I'm sure she's

worried."

"She died many years ago. Cancer."

"I'm sorry," was all he could say. All those years walking in and around the rot and shadow of death and he still couldn't find the right words to soothe the afflicted.

"It's alright. She isn't suffering anymore," she said.

"Yeah. She's in a better place," Devereux said.

"If you mean Heaven, I don't believe in it. But yes, any place is better than this city."

He looked at her. She forced a smile. It was a dig at the city; a dose of dark humor. He forced a laugh to let her know they were on the same page. It came out awkward, even by his standards. She took to it with a slight smirk.

Lily wiggled out of her leather jacket and draped it over his office chair. She leaned against the desk and crossed her arms. She was a short, thin woman with curves. Not like most petite women at all. She wore a black tank top and she was still decked out in the same wrinkled, hip-hugging jeans from the night before. She was Filipina, he could tell without even having to ask; the particular Asiatic look of her almond-shaped eyes, her compact nose, the Spanish surname.

"This city has seen better days, yes. At least that's what the history books say. Unfortunately, I was born after that timeline. My father used to say Los Angeles still had a sprinkle of magic when he got here. Before it became what you see around you."

"Your father? Where was he from?"

"He migrated here from France when he was fifteen. Actually, he was a stowaway on a cargo ship. Snuck his way inside a storage unit containing cheap wine. He left just before the war broke out and the stream of trade ships slowed to a trickle. He arrived in New York, a drunk and penniless teenager, and hitchhiked his way to Los Angeles just the same. That's where he met my mother. She came from a second-generation Mexican-American family, though she never learned Spanish."

"You're a mutt?" Lily asked. "Me too. See my skin?" She said pointing to the light complexion of her arms. "I think I have

Spanish blood in me."

"We're mutts," Devereux said. "A beautiful byproduct of our fucked-up world."

Lily brushed a few strands of hair from her eyes and smiled. "Me and my Mother were stowaways, too. We came from the city of Ilagan, in the Philippines. We crossed over on a fishing boat. It's been twelve years now."

Devereux nodded. "Not just mutts, but stowaway plague rats depending on which politician you talk to. And your father?"

"He left my mother when I was very young."

Devereux ran a hand through his short hair. "We have a lot in common. My dad died when I was eight. Drug overdose. Left my mom and my brother Robert all alone."

"Is your brother a policeman, too?"

He looked at the floor and fidgeted with his tie again. "My brother is… I don't know where he is. He ran away when he was seventeen. That's fifteen years ago now."

"I'm so sorry, she said. She sat on the opposite end of the couch leaving a gap between them. It felt like a gulf to Devereux. "I'm sure he's fine."

"It's okay. On my days off I still try to look for him. I check the local food banks or soup kitchens, hoping I'll run into him. On occasion, depending how I'm feeling, I check the morgue for John Does. Part of me just hopes he stayed out of trouble. Maybe he took a bus somewhere and started a new life. Either way, I keep looking. You'd think after all these years I'd hang it up, right?"

She reached across and planted an unusually cold hand over his.

"Your hand is cold," he said.

She closed her eyes.

Just then it hit him. He was an idiot. He'd forgotten her hands were prosthetic. Cybernetic implants. She could pulverize every bone in his body if she'd wanted to. Or if she was made to. Samuels had said that was impossible now. But what was ever a certainty in life?

She tried to pull her hand away. Devereux clasped it and

held it. "I'm sorry, Lily. I forgot."

She pulled her hand at first. Then she stopped. A thin smile flashed across her face. "I guess that's a good thing, right?"

"I suppose it is."

"There are times when I start to forget, too."

She looked around the room. She spotted his computer terminal bathing the wall in its green light. "I'm sorry, was I interrupting something?"

"No. Just finishing up my final accounts for the report. I'm off the case. It's going completely to Homicide now. I'm Vice so, it's out of my hands now."

"No," she gasped. "They can't. You have to help me. You have to help the other women."

"Kinneman is Homicide, he'll be on board. I can set up a line between you guys, if you should need anything…"

She turned away and nodded. Lily had been taking to everything pretty well considering the circumstances. A strength lived inside her that he admired. She was a mystery to him. Who was she? Just someone who popped into his world by dreadful chance? He wanted to ask about her life, her goals, but thought better of it. No point bringing that up at this point. For both their sakes.

She closed her eyes and rubbed her temples. The pain was coming back. The migraines had been more frequent now; a result of her brain rejecting whatever trash had been implanted in there.

"What's going to happen to me now?" She asked in a soft voice.

He hadn't expected that question. The room fell silent. He didn't know what to say to her. The last few hours were marked by questions he couldn't answer. Answers that had been lost in the void that was Los Angeles. He couldn't remember the last time he felt so powerless to help.

"I don't know, Lily," he said. "I don't know."

He turned to her. She had fallen asleep. It had been a long night for both of them. She had the right idea, though. Devereux reached for her cold hand and interlaced his fingers between hers. He closed his eyes and hoped the darkness would take them both away for a little while.

***

CHAPTER EIGHTEEN

SHE WOKE UP TO numbness where her forearms should have been. She turned to see Devereux asleep and holding her hand. She quickly pulled it away. Doctor Samuels had told her that her sense of touch wouldn't register as well with her new prosthetics. Phantom Limb was something she'd heard him say. The feeling that your limbs are still there, connected to you long after they're gone. She tried not to think of it.

Lily walked to the window and opened the blinds. The sun had begun its descent below the horizon as it sank below the Pacific Ocean. The endless twinkle of city lights could be seen again as the sky became dark purple.

How long had she been asleep?

The line of end-of-day traffic lights dotted the looping freeways below as they weaved in and around the city. She leaned her forehead against the window pane and looked down. All the people looked like ants from up here as an ocean of black specks swept across the city streets.

It had now been a full day since everything happened. Her audition. Her life. Everything was gone.

Not gone. Taken. She reached for the cross at her neck. Nothing. That's right, that's gone, too. *Sorry, Mom, I let you down.*

Her mother had sacrificed everything so Lily could have a better life, and now she was facing the end of that, too. Lily wanted to make her mother proud. She thought about the audition again. Her big break didn't turn out so well. It never even came. She was instead cast as an actress in a killer's perverted scheme. To think, she could've replaced the great Monica Yoshida.

A deep sinking feeling in the pit of her stomach.

Monica Yoshida.

That's right. She was there. Slumped in a dark corner all pale-skinned and blue-lipped. The woman was naked, the signs of bloat starting to set in.

"Audric," she whimpered as the images flashed in her mind. "Audric, wake up. Wake up!"

Devereux stirred. He opened his eyes; they had a glassy appearance to them as he looked around, confused. He was as shocked as she was. He looked at his watch.

"Fuck," he said standing. "It's already seven."

"Audric, I remembered something. Monica Yoshida."

"Yoshida? The actress?" He rubbed his eyes, still fighting off the grogginess.

"She was there. She was with me when I was kidnapped."

"Okay, that's something," he scrambled for the notepad on his desk. "What else can you remember?"

"She's dead. I mean, she was already dead when I got there."

Devereux pursed his lips in frustration. He turned to the wall and eyed it like he was ready to spring in and lash out at it. Instead, he nodded his head.

"I'm sorry, it just came to me."

"It's okay. This might help us."

"How?"

"LAPDOG, look into Monica Yoshida's address."

"Yoshida, Monica," a cold voice spoke from hidden speakers on his terminal screen. Lily had never seen or heard anything like it before. "Two-One-One Flower Street."

"That's not too far from Skid Row," Devereux said. "Lily you live by Skid Row, don't you? I looked up your file when you were admitted into the hospital."

"Yes."

"Computer, last known whereabouts of Ms. Yoshida."

"Last seen Tuesday night by her roommate Cantrell, Jenny, as she walked to the local grocery store. Has since been reported missing."

Something buzzed. He reached into his pocket. His phone pulsed with blinking notification lights. Devereux scanned his phone with furrowed brows.

"What is it, Audric?"

He looked up at her. "Got a message from Kinneman an hour ago. A woman was reportedly kidnapped and hauled off into a white van near her home by... Skid Row. Her mother called it in to police just a few hours ago. When the report was filed, it triggered a keyword in our databanks."

"Which word?"

"*White van.* Our computer system actively looks for keywords associated with active investigations. Word finally got back to Homicide."

"That's what happened to me," she said.

"Yeah. I'm starting to see a pattern. I'll bet the bastard's stomping ground is in your neck of the woods. Gotta be. It's a seedy part of town, right? It's possible he might've known your routines, or been keeping an eye on you. What better place to nab a girl no one would ever care about than where it's a common, everyday occurrence?"

"Is there any way you can find a record of all the white vans in Los Angeles?"

"No, that would take too much time. There has to be something else to help us narrow the search, some bit of information to cross-reference."

"Is there anything that could help?"

"I had a few theories but nothing solid. I mean, the RATs said there was a second address in Los Angeles receiving the skin shipments from Dermalab. What if it's a Paradigm employee? They have the funding, the resources, it's what they do for God's sake. What if our guy's been doing in his co-workers at Paradigm? Maybe even a former employee? That means he would have intimate knowledge of his co-workers' naughty, after-work endeavors. Maybe we could cross reference the employee databank at Paradigm and look up their registered vehicles. It's worth a damn good shot. I'll forward the idea to Kinneman or whoever's in charge right now."

"Can't you do it?"

"Like I said, I'm out. Homicide has full lead on this one."

Lily looked at his terminal. "I see you haven't finished sending your report, Audric. That means you still have a foot in the door, right? Maybe there's still something you can add to it," Lily said.

"I didn't take you for a rule-breaker Ms. Santos."

"Sometimes you have to play the part."

He smiled. "Indeed."

She felt moisture in her nose. Warm fluid trickled down into her lip.

"You're bleeding, Lily."

She wiped the moisture with the back of her hand. "Oh," was all she managed to say. Lily took a step, stumbled, and planted a hand on the desk to keep her from falling.

Devereux caught her and eased her down onto the chair. Her arms started to tremble. The shakes spread to her neck as she turned to him.

"Fuck. I'm sorry I dragged you along," Devereux said. "I should've left you at the hospital. Let's get you back. Samuels can get another look at you."

"No," she said waving him off. "There isn't much time. We have to find him."

"Lily, I..."

He didn't know what to say.

She took a breath and swept a shaky hand across her head, clearing a wavy clutter of hair away from her face. "Let me help you. I need to see this man. I'll know him when I do." She closed her eyes and exhaled slowly out her nostrils. She managed to stop the shaking.

Devereux nodded. "Alright," he said letting out a defeated breath. "You see that building there? The big, oppressive chrome one?"

Lily looked out the window. A tall, geometric wonder stood high above the adjacent monoliths of industry. The city lights warped into odd shapes as they reflected off its chrome and glass surface, creating an intoxicating show of color. The building stood like a giant prism. But for all its beauty something about the building unsettled her.

"That's Paradigm Tower, home of Paradigm Industries. They create state-of-the-art technology for the military. When wars break out and people die, their stocks go up. That's who we're dealing with." He rubbed the bridge of his nose with his thumb and forefinger. Frustration painted his worn face. "We don't have many options right now. This investigation keeps bumping into wall after wall. We're going to march down there and ask them to show us their employee records. We'll see how they play their hand."

She wiped the rest of the blood from her nose and nodded. "And me? I guess you want to bring me back to the hospital?"

Devereux smiled again. It made her feel safe.

"You're coming with me."

"Is that allowed?"

"I'm probably going to get suspended, maybe even lose my job. I don't know. I don't think that matters right now. Not when so many lives are on the line. Besides, you're my lucky charm."

Lily nodded. She thought about arguing with him. She didn't want him to lose his career over bringing her along. But she knew there were times when other things mattered more.

Devereux grabbed his coat, smiled, and walked out of the office. A death sentence. That was her verdict, but she couldn't help but smile. Maybe it was the feeling of being wanted, like she was important. An ocean of people out there, and she mattered. Maybe, after all, Mother would be proud of her.

Before she closed the door behind her, she looked out the window again. Paradigm Tower. Lily's smile faded. She took a deep breath and chased after Devereux.

Outside, the last traces of sunlight sank below the horizon, and night took hold of the city.

***

CHAPTER NINETEEN

THE LOS ANGELES METROPOLITAN Police Station sat in the heart of the city, not more than a mile away from Paradigm Industries. They had decided to walk there, as much for practicality's sake as to get the blood flowing after a long bout of sleep. They walked under the shadows of the downtown spires, Lily rubbernecking at the bright marvels like a nocturnal bug quenching its thirst for light.

"I've never been here," she said. "All these years and I've never had a reason to. It's so beautiful. It's a different experience just being underneath them."

"I'm guessing Ilagan is nothing like this?"

"No. Not even close. Rural city. All mountains and sheet metal shantytowns. Manila on the other hand is just like this, but everything is crammed together and the traffic is unbearable."

"Yeah, sounds like Los Angeles. How was life under Red Crescent rule?"

"I don't remember much anymore. The Chinese arm of the Red Crescent had already claimed the island before I was born. I do remember everyone being afraid when they would see the red uniforms walk by. I know there were curfews and there were silly stories about the soldiers eating orphaned children, but I think those were just meant to frighten them into staying out of trouble. When I left, I heard about resistance fighters trying everything to make life harder for them, like jamming enemy radar signals, or crashing their computers. Some of the resistance fighters were women who slept with the invaders, cutting their throats while they slept."

"I guess we're lucky we don't have it that bad yet. They

bombed Philadelphia when I was a kid, and Hawaii became a bloody battleground. I guess the only war I've ever seen is the one we lose every day on our streets. Poverty, inflation, drugs. Plenty of that to go around. After the economy tanked, a wave of conservative measures got voted into law, doing away with government regulation and ethics boards. Anything to give big business a shot in the arm. That's when the wage gap became a wage abyss. Homelessness was off the charts after that. Not just here, but everywhere. The government in its infinite wisdom decided to pass the Urban Recruitment Law that allowed police to scoop up and draft any homeless person it deemed capable of fighting."

"That sounds like slavery. Was it even worth it? Are we even winning the war with the Red Crescent?"

Devereux wasn't sure, he'd stopped keeping up with current events after the news cycled over and over on the daily. "I don't know."

It was almost eight o'clock and the Saturday night party crowds had started to infest the streets as they ventured for their next sensory experience. The traffic slowed to a crawl as cars looked for parking, many stationing themselves illegally on driveways and busy embankments.

The first hints of techno music bumped in the distance as the clubs began to open for business. Devereux caught a glimpse of Lily as she nodded her head to the rhythm. He had yet to see her this loose, especially after what had happened only twenty-four hours prior.

"You into this stuff?"

She looked at him with the caution of a suspect watching their words at an interrogation. "Yes. Why?"

"No reason. Didn't think you'd be into it."

"Why is that, Audric?"

"I don't know. Just didn't get that sense. I was thinking maybe Classical music or even some light K-Pop."

She crinkled her nose, as if the air took on a foul stench. "Yuck. Boring stuff. You obviously don't know me yet," she said.

He didn't say anything back. He wondered how much

time he'd actually have to get to know her. After Robert left home, it became difficult for him to make any kind of significant social bond. Friends, partners, it was like a deep-rooted dread; attachments he feared would be ripped away from his clutches and scattered to the wind. The thought of old, brittle wallpaper in an atomic blast came to mind.

"You're right, I don't know you. Last night, today, it's all been so surreal." He didn't usually make friends with people actively involved in a case. What the hell? "Tell me about yourself."

She hesitated. The question caught her off guard. "I, uh, don't know where to begin."

"Tell me what you do for a living."

"Okay. I'm a model for small clothing lines."

"Is that something you've always wanted to do?"

"No. I don't have any skills this country considers important. My body pays the bills."

"I'm sorry, Lily." He didn't know what to say to that, social ques and etiquette had always made him stumble. There was never a moment that he wasn't socially awkward.

"It's fine, Audric. The work keeps me alive and for that I am grateful. Thank you for asking."

"Sure. Why don't you tell me what you do want to do?"

"I want to be… wanted to be, I should say, an actress. I was taking night classes, method acting, dialog, all that stuff."

"You would've been great."

Lily turned away from a neon sign on a window blinking its Sanskrit text. The light from the sign washed her face in a bright purple light, illuminating the moisture in her eyes. "Thank you for making this experience easier than it might've been, Audric."

"I wish I knew how."

"Because you care."

"It's just my job."

She planted a kiss on his cheek.

He felt his face flush and his heart rate bump.

"Your face is red, Audric."

"My blood pressure is elevated. Must be stressed out."

"Is that what it is?" She asked.

He turned away from her. He was afraid. For her. For the future. For the first time in a long time, his heart ached from something other than walking up a flight of stairs or electronic interference.

Devereux fixed his gaze on the building down the block. It almost *was* the whole block. The building was some sort of Modern-Gothic hybrid all sleek and sullen. He pictured Dracula in his three-piece suit peering down from the highest window, licking his black lips as his cattle wandered dumbly below. In the ages to come, thought Devereux, when all the civilizations had long turned to dust, this building would stand above the ruins, like the ancient temples of Mexico, or the pyramids of Egypt.

"Well, looks like we're here."

"It's a scary building," she said, wrapping her arms around herself.

"You're not wrong. It's where Boogeymen scheme in efficient warfare. They specialize in biotechnology, like stem cells that heal wounds as fast as they're made, or weaponized viruses that make the host's body attack itself. They invented the neural flechette. You'd think with all the creative ways we've thought up how to kill people, this war would've been over by now." He looked at the building. "It seems like it's been perpetual, like the rise and fall of the sun."

"I don't remember a day in the Philippines without the bombs exploding on the black horizon over the ocean at night."

"I don't remember a day when a small cup of coffee was less than ten dollars. Pure evil. Wars'll do that, too. Life gets cheaper but not your coffee."

They walked to the front where large rectangular glass doors framed the lobby entrance. A woman at the desk waved at him and buzzed the door open.

Inside, a red carpet led to the information desk where the woman sat at her multi-screen terminal, finger-tapping every monitor like a punk rock drummer. The room was a spacious, high-ceilinged lobby built in some neo-Art Deco style. Intricate geometric patterns decorated the walls and ceiling in that twentieth century New York Gothic style he'd seen in the old black and whites on the Holoscreen. The décor gave off the impression of class and power; modern and sleek on the outside, vintage and prestigious on the inside. It echoed what the men and women who worked inside its halls probably felt.

He approached the woman at the desk and flipped his badge. "Detective Devereux. Vice. I'd like to speak to your CEO, Werner Heinrich. I need to browse employee records in relation to multiple homicides I'm investigating."

The woman flashed a fake smile sharp as steel, polished time and time again after dealing with all the imbeciles that walked through the lobby. She apparently thought he fit the bill.

"Very well, Detective. Do you have a warrant or perhaps an appointment?"

"Nope. Call him."

She frowned and whispered into a mouthpiece.

Lily looked around, taking in all the sights. She was careful not to touch anything, keeping her hands close to her sides as if the room was contaminated. He could tell she wasn't comfortable being inside the belly of the monolith. She hovered close to him as a pair of tall security guards walked by decked out in new pressed suits and high-tech sunglasses. He knew what they were just by looking at them. The glasses transmitted live closed circuit video feed, allowing the men to become mobile surveillance drones. The guards eyed them both before they disappeared into a door behind the information desk.

"Mister Heinrich has granted you access," the woman said.

"Thank you. He still in the building?"

"Yes, he has a residence here along with many members of the board. He happens to be working late tonight and has agreed to see you and…" The woman paused, eyeing Lily up and down as if she were trash in a jacket.

"This is my partner, Detective Santos. She just got back from some undercover surveillance work."

"Very well. Hundredth floor. Room One-oh-five B. Elevator

is right over there to your left."

"Much obliged."

They summoned the elevator. When the doors closed, Devereux breathed a sigh of relief.

"Audric, what are you doing?"

"You're an actress, right? Think of it as your next role."

"I don't know what to do."

"Don't say anything and start looking around."

Lily raised an eyebrow. "Start looking around?"

"Yeah, like you're observing his office, his clothes. Don't just stand still, detectives are always looking around, always scrutinizing something. And look mean."

She nodded and furrowed her brows. Her lips became a rigid line.

"Good enough," he said.

The ride up the elevator seemed to last an eternity. The walls were polished glass, their reflections staring back at them. Heavy bags had developed under his eyes and his stubble had grown a considerable amount since he'd shaved Friday morning. His skin was pale and his lips were cracking like an arid desert. He thought he was staring at a living corpse.

"Who is Heinrich?" Lily asked.

He turned away from his reflection. "Werner Heinrich, Chief Executive Officer of Paradigm Industries. He single-handedly brought Paradigm out of the ruins and turned it into the corporation you see today. Mostly by redirecting tech away from the public sector and focusing it on the war. Investing in chaos nets you some good returns."

"Unless it's the chaos on the streets."

"Right. I hear he's ruthless. Let me do the talking."

Lily nodded with a trace of nervousness in her face.

"Don't worry. Worst that can happen is we'll get escorted out the building. I hope."

The doors opened. A wide hallway greeted them. It appeared to be a labyrinth of private offices and boardrooms. This was where the high rollers worked, where the men and women who ran the machine stalked the hallways during the day.

The door to room 105B was different than the rest. Fancy stuff: a heavy mahogany door, polished top to bottom, with brass handles shaped like lions. Dracula's lair. Devereux knocked. A moment passed before the door buzzed open.

The office was spacious; it could've housed three families in its soothingly cool interior. Inside: wooden floors and black leather chairs; top-of-the-line terminals, Holoscreens, and portable surveillance devices. Any sap lucky enough to pawn the stuff would've made a killing.

Heinrich stood behind his desk. He was a tall man with a perfect posture and broad shoulders. He had neatly buzzed silver hair and a perfectly trimmed beard lining his mouth. The expensive blue suit he wore was probably tailored somewhere in Europe and must have cost a small fortune alone in shipping costs. His face was unnaturally smooth and stretched out. Devereux noted the minuscule incisions on his jowls, a patchwork of near flawless plastic surgery procedures. The man was pushing his late seventies and he barely looked a day over fifty. Heinrich had bribed away the effects of time.

"To what do I owe this honor, Detective…?" He said extending a hand. His voice was loud, powerful, not unlike a lion's roar.

"Devereux," he said shaking his hand. Heinrich's hand was large, his cold, long fingers almost wrapping entirely around Devereux's hand. "This is my partner Detective Santos."

Lily nodded and smiled politely as she stood behind Devereux.

"Welcome, the both of you. Now how exactly can I be of assistance?"

"We are investigating the recent string of homicides that befell three of your employees, as well as one of their personal drivers. We have a lead we'd like to follow up on and I'd like to take a look at your files. Employee records to be exact."

"I see," said Heinrich. "Such a tragic series of events in the last twenty-four hours. It's shaken up the entire company. All exceptional men. What exactly is your lead, if I may ask?"

"I'd rather not say as the investigation is still ongoing. I'd just like to cross-reference your database with city files. I will say we may be on the verge of a breakthrough."

Heinrich nodded and walked up to Devereux, placing his hands behind his back; he stood at least six inches taller, and in another life, Devereux might have been intimidated. "So, let me get this straight. You come in here without a warrant, you ask for unrestricted access to my employee database, and you bring your girlfriend along, all while withholding information from me?"

Lily blushed.

"Detective Santos and I aren't- "

"I think you can cut the act, Detective. I have retinal scanners embedded in the lobby walls. I knew who you both were the second you walked in here."

Devereux turned to Lily and back to Heinrich. "This is Lily Santos. Did your retinal scanners tell you she was a victim in this case?"

Heinrich raised an eyebrow.

"She was kidnapped by our killer and used to murder two of your former employees. Have your attention yet?"

"Is this a joke, Detective?"

"No. This woman underwent a neural procedure that allowed her thoughts and actions to be controlled by a remote operator. She isn't the only one. She saw the corpses of more women, just like her. They were all part of some twisted experiment. Now, if you don't help me, more people will die."

Heinrich stood quiet as he considered the information. He turned to look at Lily. "In what ways was she used?"

"Why don't you ask her yourself?"

"Forgive me, Miss Santos, I-"

"I was raped, Mister Heinrich. By your employees. I was bait."

"I don't understand."

"What don't you follow, Heinrich?" Devereux said, agitated. "Your guys were chasing tail on the nightly. Whoever our killer is knew that, kidnapped women off the street, controlled them, and had them kill your boys. Shall I describe how each of them died?"

"That won't be necessary," Heinrich said, glaring at Devereux.

"Let me tell you something else. Miss Santos is dying; her brain is rejecting the implants in her head. I have reason to believe it may have been one of your former employees. You guys do like to dabble in this kind of stuff, don't you?"

Heinrich walked to his desk and sat in his chair. He let out a deep sigh. In that moment, he looked tired; not at all the big intimidating lion from moments before.

Devereux approached his desk. "You already knew, didn't you?"

"I—" Heinrich paused, "—had a fear."

"Former employees. Someone who was fired or had an agenda. Someone with intimate knowledge of his co-workers and their vices. Tell me."

"I can't be sure. But I may have an idea. He wasn't fired. He quit. Under protest."

"Of what? Who?"

"A secret project. It was our next phase in an experimental military procedure. Mind control."

Lily walked closer to both men. She looked at Heinrich in what Devereux assumed was anger.

"Control Theory," Devereux said.

Heinrich looked up. His eyebrows arched and his lips curved downward as his plastic face mustered up its best expression of shock the surgery would allow.

"How did you know that?"

"I have friends in low places, Mister Heinrich. Very low places."

Heinrich folded his hands together on his desk. He nodded. There was no fighting this one. "We were developing neural implants we could insert into captured enemy combatant brains along with a Brain Computer Interface for easy monitoring. The idea was to send them back out into the field, back into enemy hands, and enhance our surveillance methods."

"Controlled spying," Devereux said.

"Yes. And there was another phase, a much more…questionable phase, if you will. Paradigm had also successfully developed prosthetic limbs during a previous project. Virtually unidentifiable from real flesh and bone, they could be surgically fused onto any test subject with no one being the wiser. These prosthetics could crush steel; withstand large amounts of pressure and damage. Ultimately, we decided to combine both projects, enhancing captured troops with mind control implants in tandem with our artificial limbs. So, when we did send out our spies, and we happened to identify an important target, we could theoretically… liquidate said target."

"Mind control, spying, and assassinations. Paradigm's full of sick bastards, isn't it? Who then? Who's responsible?"

"I didn't know our employees were being murdered by women undergoing cerebral manipulation, but it's so obvious now. How else could they get so close, so quickly? Anton Daneker," he said shaking his head. "A very troubled man."

"How do you know?"

"He was a bioconservative."

"A what?"

"A bioconservative. Someone who takes a stand against body augmentations or modifications through the use of technology. They are as old-fashioned as they come."

Devereux furrowed his brows. "That doesn't make sense, Heinrich. Our guy's using this technology freely."

"He didn't start out that way. He was our Chief Research Officer for Project Descartes, the precursor to Project Control Theory. He didn't start with the company, but he was a leading neural engineer, so we brought him onboard. For unexplained reasons, he had a change of heart and felt that all our testing was immoral, unethical. He spoke openly against it to the board, but we refused to listen. Our finances had taken a dive and we felt the project was the future of espionage and warfare. We needed to sell the project to the Pentagon. We had invested too much into it at that point. The project, the board decided, would continue. Shortly after, he dismissed himself, leaving with much of the project knowledge. We had notes and leading researchers still working on it, even as far as testing it on a few subjects, but he was tops in his field. After he left, the project stalled, took on failed iterations, and eventually the military lost patience with us and invested its surveillance budget on unmanned drones. And that was that."

Lily turned to Devereux. "Why would he be using the technology when he is so openly against it?"

"I don't know. Was he religious, Heinrich? Psychological problems?"

"I'm not sure. I do know many bioconservatives tend to have a theological leaning. Sometimes their religion comes into conflict with science. *God is against technology* sort of banter."

"Sounds like he's punishing people," Devereux said. "He's punishing the company, using their own creations against its employees; the people that refused to accept his dogma. All while using defenseless women as test subjects and bait. Heinrich, I need to access your computer. I must cross-reference something. Let me do this."

Heinrich pursed his lips as if pondering the hardest decision, he ever had to make. He stood up and motioned at his desk with a sweep of his hand. "Please, please."

Devereux approached Heinrich's terminal and swiped his I.D. He accessed the city's registry banks, where all general information on Los Angeles' residents could be found. He prompted Anton Daneker into the query box, and everything the man ever was popped up on a screen; he was forty-eight, six-feet tall, one-hundred-sixty pounds. Originally from Sacramento, California, he moved across the U.S. taking on different private projects until Paradigm came knocking. Devereux checked his DMV records and pulled a list of registered cars and parking citations.

"No major crimes or convictions, only minor traffic and parking citations; one as recent as a week ago for parking in a red zone. The vehicle registered was a white, twenty-ten Ford van. There is no record of it having been in an accident and-"

Devereux turned to Lily. "This might be it, Lily," he said

jabbing a finger at the monitor. "His address lists him a few blocks from your apartment. It's not a house, though. It appears to be a defunct auto garage. That sounds like an ideal workspace for the kinda shit that's been going on, wouldn't you say?"

Lily nodded her head. "Take me with you. I can remember him if I see him or take a look inside the garage."

"Lily, I don't want to put you in a dangerous situation."

"I don't have long to live. We both know that. If he's got other women under the knife, they won't either."

"Lily, I have to call this in, but it might take a while for a judge to approve a warrant, considering our recent fiasco with Fontaine. I can only go on investigative purposes and maybe question neighbors. I don't know how much help you can be."

"I have to be there. Please just let me do this. Let the end of my life have some value."

"It already has value."

"Then let's show that woman he just kidnapped how valuable *she* really is."

Devereux smiled. She was a wizard, the way she could convince him of anything. Or was he letting her?

"Alright, but you're staying in the car."

Devereux walked toward the door. Heinrich faced Lily. "I'm sorry about what happened to you, Ms. Santos. I had no idea something like this would happen. It's regrettable to find that our project worked so well in this…fashion. I will have my top men look into making you right. I hope you find him soon."

Lily nodded and walked out into the hallway. Devereux turned to Heinrich before he stepped out the door. "Before it was renamed Control Theory, why was it called Project Descartes?"

Heinrich sat back in his chair. He pulled out a thick leather book from inside a drawer. The book was worn and tattered from years of exposure. The title of the book was Great Western Philosophers. "Philosopher René Descartes theorized that it was possible that a person would never know if an evil demon had trapped his mind in a black box only to control every input and output of his life."

"Guess that makes you guys the demons," Devereux said.

Heinrich pressed his lips together and turned away to face the window. He stared at the crowds and lights below. The lair of Dracula indeed.

Devereux unholstered his sidearm and checked the clip. He switched the safety off and ran to catch up to Lily.

***

CHAPTER TWENTY

THE DATABANK LISTED ANTON Daneker's address as 1132 Winston Street. Devereux remembered a few assignments in that part of town. Dealers there slanged out in the open and teenage call girls strutted up and down the dirty sidewalks. Living beside them: the people with mortgages and down-and-out artists scrambling just to make rent. They all had to cope with each other on a daily, like a zoo without cages. The area was collectively part of what was known as L.A.'s Skid Row. When an officer was tasked with an assignment there, usually it involved them doing something to piss off the Watch Commander. The philosophy was that it was just best to let the garbage pile up and let them weed each other out.

Devereux saw the address and parked across the street. The place was an abandoned car garage with a second-floor apartment space above it. In a faded blue cursive font, the garage read Ricardo's Tire Service. There was no sign of a van, neither parked on the lot nor on the street. Devereux assumed it was either stationed inside the building or the bastard was on the prowl.

The building adjacent to the garage was a run-down single story apartment complex. He'd decided that he'd start by asking the neighbors some questions. He took a breath and tapped his chest. He caught Lily looking at him.

"Cardiac resynchronization. It regulates the electric signals in my heart's chambers. Keeps it pumping."

Lily gave him a grim look. He wasn't sure if it was fear or sadness.

"It's kind of nifty. The device is really a sleeve that goes over my heart. It's got all these nodes that conduct electric impulses."

"The technology inside you is keeping you alive and what's inside of me is killing me. When did the world come to this?"

Devereux looked out the windshield. What were once smoothly-paved streets were now pock-marked with potholes. The litter of fast food wrappers filled the vents of the storm drains below. The world was eroding before him, leaving only the grimy skeleton of what was once the City of Angels. "It's not keeping me alive so much as slowing my death. It's never been easy for me. It's not something I ever talk about, but I don't expect to see the next decade. The gears are slowly grinding to a halt. The device can only do so much, but it can't keep resuscitating a decaying organ. I can't afford an artificial heart. I'm not influential enough to be on the organ donor list. The world of the future belongs to those who built it. In that world, I'm nothing more than a sanitation worker. Before the War, there were stories about how it was an age of scientific miracles. Now, all this technology around us and we get lost in the scramble to make better weapons and not better people. Now we build long-lasting wind-up motors instead of long lasting wind-up hearts. Pretty soon the weapons we create will outlive their makers. Lily, when we catch this guy, we'll know exactly what he did to you, to the others. We'll find a way, I promise."

She put her cold hand on his arm and smiled. He smiled back. They were both in their own personal way dying. But between them, a mutual respect and understanding. They would fight until the end. Devereux knew: in the carcass of the rotting city, a heart still beat.

"I'm gonna go ask around. I need you to stay in the car. I've already called in my request for a warrant. When that gets approved, backup will get here."

"I can go with you. I think it's him, Audric. If I see him or the van, I will know."

"Sorry, Lily. If it is him, we don't know what to expect. All of this, it's something I've never dealt with."

Lily nodded. Devereux reached into his coat and pulled out his notepad. "Here. Take this and write down anything strange you see. It'll keep your mind off things for a while. Okay?"

She took the pad and smiled. "Yes, boss."

He stepped outside. The night had turned unusually cold. He took off his coat and gave it to Lily. "Take this too, it's getting cold." He winked and closed the door.

As he crossed the street, a transient dressed in rags with plastic bags for shoes pushed two shopping carts full of cans. The rag-mummy turned to Devereux and said, "The system got me. Don't let it get you too." He laughed as he pushed his armada of carts into the night.

He came to 1130 Winston Street, a low-rent apartment complex with a broken sprinkler spraying a dead lawn. The apartment had been barricaded with iron bars along the door and windows. He rang the buzzer. Devereux turned to his right and looked at the empty garage parking lot. After a moment, a Hispanic man came to the door. "What do you want?"

"I'm with the Los Angeles Police Department." He flashed his badge. "I'm Detective Audric Devereux, and I have some questions I'd like to ask you. May I get your name?"

The man looked at the badge and at Devereux's face. "Victor Ayala. But I don't know anything, don't see anything, and I keep to myself. Now, leave."

"It's not about you or anyone who lives here. It's about your neighbor over there," Devereux said, tilting his head at the garage.

"I don't know him."

"Are you sure? His name is Anton Daneker. He's listed as living in that address."

Ayala looked at the garage and said, "I don't know his name. I have to go."

"Maybe you know what he drives? Does he have a white van?"

The man sighed and nodded his head.

"Great. Now, sir, did you happen to notice any damage to the car? A dent, maybe?"

"He told me he wouldn't get his insurance involved. We took care of this."

"It's fine. I don't care about that. Just tell me what happened."

"I didn't see him. I hit him; it was an accident. I wasn't drinkin' or nothin'. We didn't want to make a big deal; no police, no insurance. I paid him. If he didn't get it fixed, that's his fault, but I paid him. Fuck that fool."

"You're okay. Get back inside, and thanks for your help."

Devereux reached for his cell. He'd recorded the whole conversation. California law allowed for secret recordings by law enforcement officers; it was legal and admissible in court. He messaged Ayala's testimony to Kinneman and told him to register it as evidence. He had strong reason to believe now that the van that Lily had witnessed on the night of her abduction was the same one registered to Anton Daneker, ex-Paradigm employee who quit under moral objection to his experimental work at Paradigm Industries. Experimental work which was identical to what doctors found on Lily's body. He hoped the search warrant would get approved on grounds of probable cause.

He wasn't sure if it was the cold air or his nerves, but Devereux's hands trembled. If it came to it, he hoped he could still pull off a straight shot.

He walked casually towards Daneker's address. The parking lot was an empty space of cracked cement and oil slicks. The lamps that hung above the property had long burned out, leaving that part of the block in darkness. Old axle grease stains lined the pavement where cars were once serviced along the side of the road. Ricardo's Tires had fallen into the economic sinkhole of many small businesses that had become refuge to squatters, crack heads, and other assorted fiends. This one in particular felt that he was above the law; that he was God himself. A puppet master pulling at the strings of his marionettes; a deadly dance involving the life of innocent lives.

His phone vibrated. Kinneman. The warrant received the green light. *Do not proceed without backup, already on route.*

He looked at Lily as she sat in the car. She buried her head in both her hands. The migraines. Whatever was in her head was eating away at her from the inside. No time. Fuck that. He was going in.

He approached the garage door and pulled out his pistol. A tangle of clipped wires hung below the card reader like dead snakes. It had been illegally deactivated. No way to open the door. He had to look for another way.

He circled to the rear of the building. Above, the fire escape ladder hung just out of reach. Above the ladder, a narrow catwalk led to a small window. If he could reach it, he could try to pry it open. It was worth a shot.

Devereux hopped up and just managed to catch onto a rusted ladder rung. He pulled himself up and climbed up the catwalk. He peered through the window but saw only his reflection. Sweat had started to form like little beads on his face. Devereux jiggled the window latch. The clasp was stuck from years of inactivity. The Fire Department had stopped making routine inspections on places like this years ago after a slashed city budget.

With a heave, he lifted the window and a smattering of dust blew into the air. He fought off a sneeze and peered inside. Black.

His heart started to beat faster. He pulled the pistol's hammer back and crawled inside. In the distance, he heard the faint sound of sirens. No time. Inside, the air was damp; he would enter the lair of the puppet master alone and in one of the few times in his life he could remember, he felt afraid.

***

CHAPTER TWENTY-ONE

HE HEARD WATER TRICKLING somewhere in the room. He unclipped the small flashlight from his belt and turned it on. Darkness engulfed the room making it too dangerous to prowl around; he needed light even if it meant losing the element of surprise. Water splashed on his shirt, soaking through the thin fabric. He looked up. The roof had sprung multiple leaks, cascading thin streams of water from the corners of the ceiling all the way down to the walls. He wasn't sure if it was trapped rainwater or bad plumbing, but the leaks ranged from droplets, to small, steady rivulets.

Devereux found a light switch along the wall. He flicked it and nothing happened. This was apparently the place where light came to crawl away and die. Either Daneker didn't pay his bills or he wanted it this way for a reason.

The place stank. The air was charged with the smell of rot. The first time he'd smelled something similar was when his mother had found a bloated possum under the house. He came to know it as the smell of death.

His light probed the room. A dusty nightstand patrolled one corner of the room with a small tower of books craning just off the edge. The books whispered of their reader's tastes: Paradise Lost, The Inferno, Gray's Anatomy, the Bible. There were also pamphlets and chapbooks on the floor with what looked like anti-government propaganda.

A single mattress lay on the floor next to an extinguished candle. It looked like he was in the master bedroom. The rest of the room was clear.

He opened the door to the hallway and the smell of

death became more potent. His mind tried to push aside what he was suspecting. *Don't think it until you see it.* He closed his eyes and took a step into the hallway. *More dead girls, I know it.*

Distant humming filled the air, like a generator rumbling in anger. To his right, the bathroom door was open. It looked to Devereux like the bathroom mirror had been forcibly removed by the bent ridges along the medicine cabinet's frame. He shined the light on the wastebasket. Nestled among toilet tissue was a pair of blue shriveled latex gloves. They were stained red. It looked fresh. His fingers curled tighter around the butt of his gun.

Outside, the kitchen was nothing more than a small room with a compact stove. Dirty frying pans sat piled atop one another on the cracked ceramic counter. The cabinets contained canned foods; tuna, sardines, corn.

A narrow stairway led away from the kitchen and to the bottom floor. Devereux stepped lightly along the sides of the stairs to avoid unnecessary creaking. A door with a shattered bolt waited for him at the bottom of the stairs. He nudged the door open and the odor in the room nearly made him gag.

Industrial lights hung from the ceiling, dimly lighting the garage. The garage was spacious, able to possibly house eight to ten pickup trucks across, including room for machinery. A generator sat rumbling near the middle of the garage, plugged into a broken electrical socket by a thick, black cable. The garage space was a maze of workbenches, tools, and medical equipment like scalpels and bone saws. He ducked next to a small filing cabinet and looked around for any point of reference.

When Devereux was a boy his father had taken him to a haunted house on Halloween night. The house was in the style of a southern Gothic plantation house, rife with empty rocking chairs swaying back and forth, and candles bleeding wax into wooden tables. Every now and then a costumed freak would pop out and garner some cheap screams, but what scared him the most was what wasn't there— the fear of what was lying in wait in the other room. And there was never a way back; the line moved only forward.

He crouched ahead and peered around an old sawhorse. That's when he saw them. Their faces were masks of white caked-on makeup that had long dried and settled into their pores. They'd been dressed to look like living dolls. Four naked women sat bloated against the back wall. Three looked blankly at the dirty floor; a snapshot of the last image they ever saw ingrained into their brains. One, an Asian woman, looked at Devereux. Her stare was an accusatory one, making him feel the guilt of having failed her. He assumed she was Monica Yoshida, former actress, former living human being.

Toward the center of the room, a small pair of feet dangled over an operating table. He made his way quietly across. When he reached the operating table, he stood quietly. He spotted a naked woman splayed out like a corpse. He scanned the room. No sign of anyone. He looked back down at her. She lay naked in absolute tranquility. No older than twenty-one, tops. She was an attractive woman with perfectly symmetrical facial features and full red lips. Her head had been shaved unevenly, leaving small patches of hair spread across her mostly bare head. A line of wire jutted out the back of her skull. Devereux's eyes followed the connection to a portable terminal with a glitching red monitor.

Devereux looked for any vital signs on the screen. The monitor only displayed a blinking sequence of random numbers and symbols which were unfamiliar to him. The terminal had a small card entry slot. If he could commandeer the software, maybe he'd get some kind of fix on the killer's whereabouts. He swiped his card across the reader. Nothing. The terminal must have been encrypted, even from police use.

He looked back at the woman. A row of scalpels lined the top of a small tray beside her body. *Fuck.* Another one he didn't get to save in time. With his free hand, he pressed his index and middle finger into her throat to feel for a pulse.

A long moan howled as the garage door creaked open. Bright headlights cut into the room as a vehicle drove in slowly. Devereux ducked under the table and killed the flashlight. The car door slammed. Footsteps approached his direction. He sprang up, aiming his gun, "Police, put your-"

The driver was gone. The van sat idly by the maw of the open garage. The vehicle was white with a dent on the passenger-side door. The headlights tagged his shirt, making him stick out like a sore thumb. His hands trembled. He checked his sides. Nothing. Just the clutter of old machinery and rusted tools bathed in darkness. The haunted house.

A sharp pain burst inside his chest. His pacemaker was drawing interference. He clutched his chest and spun around. The woman on the operating table convulsed as if a current of power coursed through her body. Her eyes sprang open, pulsing blue lights into the dark of the garage. She shot to her feet like lightning and yanked the cable from her head. Before he could turn his weapon on her, she squeezed his hand and crushed every bone in it. He tried to scream but the pain was like a bolt of heat that traveled up his spine, shutting down all his motor functions. The singe in his nerves made jelly of his legs. His body hit the floor. He almost blacked out. Almost.

The skinhead grabbed Devereux by his hair and pulled him to his feet. She looked at him, studied him like a specimen. She placed one hand on his chin and another on his top row of teeth. Before she pulled his jaw apart, another arm shot out and gripped Skinhead's wrist. Lily stood there in her leather jacket and blue jeans looking like a wiz-bang street brawler. She whipped her hand back and a chunk of flesh and wiring ripped away from Skinhead's forearm. The woman reeled backwards. She planted her feet apart, squaring up with Lily, her blue eyes accosting her. Skinhead lunged forward and wrapped a hand around Lily's neck. Lily shot an open-palm under her attacker's chin, sending a spray of blood from her mouth into the air. Devereux crawled forward as both women became entangled in a mechanized dance of violence.

He tried to stand but his legs wobbled and he fell back on his knees. His heart bumped against his chest. Radio wave interference was scrambling his pacemaker, just like when he met Lily. He gasped for air with an open mouth, letting the hot air in the room travel down his constricted throat. Sweat poured down the sides of his face. He looked at his right hand: a mangled piece of meat, his fingers had gnarled into a twisted ball of skin and splintered bone. He probed the floor for his pistol with his left hand. Above him, the girls grabbed and clawed at each other. Blood and mechanical fluids splashed on the floor.

He unclipped the flashlight and scanned the floor with his light. His pistol had been kicked aside into the clutter and darkness.

He heard a scream. He looked up. Skinhead clawed at Lily's face, dragging skin and blood on the edges of her fingernails.

Devereux pushed off the floor with his left hand. He leaned against the operating table.

Blood ran down Lily's face, trickles of it streaming into her eyes. Her jacket had torn to ribbons as she tangled through a tempest of prosthetic fists and elbows. The naked cyborg in front of her was a specimen of brute strength and sharp reflexes.

Lily snapped a knife-edged hand strike at Skinhead's throat. The blow connected, hurtling metal into bone. The impact of the strike made the cyborg bite down on her tongue, snapping off a lump of pink flesh. A river of rich crimson cascaded down skinhead's mouth and onto her chin. She didn't seem to exhibit any signs of pain as she stared blankly ahead, the blue lights from her eyes focusing solely on Lily.

Skinhead planted her legs and bent down. She sprung forward, tackling Lily to the floor. The back of Lily's head slammed against concrete. The cyborg wrapped her left hand around Lily's jaw.

Devereux pushed off the operating table and limped forward as fast as his body would let him. A glimmer caught his attention in the corner of his eye. A row of knives and surgical tools lay splayed out on an aluminum tray. He snatched a scalpel and limped toward the women. He stood directly behind Skinhead as she plunged her right hand into Lily's mouth. Devereux raised the scalpel to the sky and came down with all the strength he could muster. The blade landed on the back of skinhead's neck, piercing pure flesh. The cyborg let go of Lily as her hands spasmed outward. She stood and turned, facing Devereux now with eyes of blue light. He took a step back. Skinhead took a single step forward. The lights in her eyes faded, revealing her natural brown irises. She looked at him in confusion for a brief moment before the life in her eyes snuffed out. She collapsed at his feet.

Devereux rushed to Lily as she writhed on the floor. With his left hand, he scooped the back of her neck and cradled her head against his chest. "Lily, are you okay?"

Lily opened her eyes. "Yes. I-I think so."

The sirens wailed closer in the distance.

"Backup is on its way," he whispered.

She nodded. Her face was a canvas of blood and slashed skin.

"You saved my life. Thank you." He put his forehead to hers and smiled. "I lost the driver," he said suddenly, remembering. "It's not safe here." Lily's face contorted as she looked behind him.

Just then he felt cold metal at the back of his head. He raised his arms. A deep, scratchy voice whispered in his ear. "I know your police friends are coming. I'm going to take my girl back, and you're going to tell your friends not to follow me. Do you understand?"

Devereux looked at Lily and nodded slowly. She was scared. He wished she could read his mind, so she could hear him say how strong he knew she was.

The man grabbed Lily by the arm and jerked her off the floor. He jabbed Devereux's pistol into Lily's temple. He was lean and gawky with a frizzled face. He hadn't shaved in weeks. The signs of fatigue and sleeplessness painted his face with dark eye circles and deep ridges around his mouth. "Get in the van," he said to Lily, never taking his eyes off Devereux. She entered the van through the passenger door.

Daneker turned the ignition and the van rumbled to life. Devereux looked into his eyes. Nothing but madness in them. The look he'd seen on murderers who didn't know the value of life. Murderers who, when confronted by the victim's family, only sat in silence, like a child who didn't understand why he'd been punished. Daneker stared back and furrowed his brows. He extended his arm out the window. A crack of thunder exploded through the garage. Devereux slumped to the floor.

***

CHAPTER TWENTY-TWO

"NO!" LILY CRIED OUT. "No, no, no, no!" A flash of rage took hold of her unlike the power any mind control could ever do. She snapped for Daneker's gun and crushed the weapon in her hand. Metal and springs flew apart.

Daneker pushed back with a force that knocked Lily's head against the passenger window. Glass shattered as the back of her head became wet. He reached for Lily's throat with blinding speed. It caught her off guard. His long fingers wrapped around her neck and squeezed. As the flow of air cut off from her lungs, she looked at him. A look of joy painted his face as he slowly sapped the life from her.

"You were my favorite, darling," he said in a familiar, coarse voice. "Now I have to end this."

It all came flooding in at once. The memories that had eluded her came surging back, twisting at her insides. He was the madman the shadows had spat out. He was the man who had asked her for the time out on the street. Daneker was the puppet master.

Lily gripped one of his fingers and snapped it upwards. Daneker released her as he howled in pain.

He struck her across the face. The taste of wet copper sloshed inside her mouth.

His green eyes turned into bright blue lights. He threw his body into her, throwing a flurry of elbows and fists. Lily struggled as he brought his power and weight down on her small frame. She looked at his chest. A silver cross hung down his neck. Mother. A deep rage boiled. Her hand probed the dashboard, feeling for any weapon. Then she remembered as she reached for her back pocket. She pulled out a small notepad with her one free hand, as the other pushed his face away. She unhooked Devereux's pencil from the notepad and thrust it into Daneker's right eye. He screamed in agony. The light of his eye flickered and died out.

Tires screeched outside the garage door. A light show of blue and red pulled up behind the van. Officers took up positions and drew their weapons.

Daneker peered into the rear-view mirror with his single blue eye. He turned to Lily, the lone light blinding her. Without saying a word, he wrapped his hand around his neck and snapped it. The sound of the crunch made Lily gasp. The light in his eye died.

A low moan came from the back of the van. Lily turned around in her seat. A woman lay naked in the back of the van, her limbs bound, her mouth gagged with a tie. The naked woman shivered as she stared at the bloodied woman in front of her. Lily forced a painful smile and said, "Everything is going to be okay, I promise."

Lily turned to look at Devereux lying in a pool of blood. She opened the door to run to him. A sharp pulse shot through her head. She placed a single foot on the ground before she collapsed. The world started to turn black. Sleep. Finally, there would be peace, she thought. There was comfort in nothingness. Maybe death wasn't that bad.

As footsteps approached, the world finally went away.

***

CHAPTER TWENTY-THREE

SHE DIDN'T REMEMBER IF she dreamt, and if she did, the dreams had vanished into that nebulous cloud of forgotten memories that was the ether. The only thing she knew was that feeling of satisfaction when woken from a long-deserved nap where time ceases to exist and a peaceful blankness envelops the consciousness.

Her eyes opened and they tried to adjust to the light. A wave of fatigue swept over her body as she tried moving her limbs. It took effort, more than it should have. Her thoughts didn't form coherently; she just felt like a camera on the wall observing things with no sense of narrative. Her location, the time, the date— she didn't know any of it.

Lily heard a voice. A familiar face appeared above her as her vision adjusted. He had messy white hair and kind blue eyes. A doctor? Yes, he was a doctor.

"Lily, I am so glad you're awake. Do you remember me? I'm Doctor Samuels."

Lily nodded and smiled.

"How are you feeling?"

Lily mouthed the word, "tired."

Samuels put his hand on her head like a good father. "You've had it rough, we know. But I am very happy to see you awake. You've been out two weeks."

She didn't quite grasp the concept of time yet and she nodded dumbly.

"You went into a coma. Your brain couldn't handle the hardware inside you and shut down. Thanks to some of the finest surgeons at Paradigm, we operated on you as quickly as possible. We retrieved the BCIs behind your eyes successfully, as well as detaching the spinal implants that relayed impulses into your nervous system. We did our best, but I'm afraid your back was left with severe scarring."

Lily looked up at the ceiling. She wasn't sure if she was apathetic or just jaded as the words just flew by her and swirled into the void of her short-term memory. He continued, "We also removed the shunt on the back of your head where Daneker inserted the control virus inside you. Unfortunately, we have no way to combat the virus; you may have to live with that for the rest of your life."

Those last words gestated in her head: The rest of your life. She wasn't sure that meant anything to her anymore. She would live? She wondered if she was still dreaming. If it were true, the scarring wasn't just on her body, it was internal, too. The scars wouldn't heal. They were ugly things she didn't want to remember. Nothing in this life could make her forget, she was sure.

"Blue light may still trigger random impulses of aggression every now and then. We recommend wearing sunglasses or dark visors to combat that problem. The outbursts can be controlled with meditation. As for the trauma of all that has happened to you, we will provide a counselor for psychological support as well but at the very least know that no one will be controlling you, Lily."

She looked down at her hands.

"We patched up the prosthetics where they were damaged. Many soldiers come back from war zones and live fully normal lives with these high-quality prosthetics."

Lily nodded and forced a smile. Small traces of tranquilizers still flowed through her bloodstream, she could tell. Everything seemed to move slowly. She looked at a clock on the wall. The gears ticked away as one hand moved forward in a circle. She looked at her hands again. They still looked real. She pinched one and felt a dull pain. She looked down and saw a flash of light at her chest. A silver cross hung on her neck. Her mother's. She felt the warm moisture descend her cheeks. *Thank you for not giving up on me, Mother.*

"Doctor?" Lily asked, not sure she wanted an answer.

"Yes?"

"How is Audric?"

Samuels lowered his head. "I'm afraid I can't disclose that to you as you are not immediate family."

Lily reached a hand out and gently tugged on his coat. "Neither of us have family," she said.

Samuels nodded. He understood. "He received a gunshot wound to the chest, the bullet just narrowly avoiding his heart. He bled extensively and was rushed to the hospital for an emergency blood transfusion. He took to it very well. He's here recovering in our inpatient wing, two floors up."

Lily smiled from ear to ear.

"I suppose you would like to see him, wouldn't you?"

"I would like that very much," she said as she reached out to hug him. She squeezed harder than she intended as Samuels yelped. "Sorry, I forgot."

"It's alright," he said, rubbing his lower spine.

Samuels had one of the nurses bring her a wheelchair. After a lengthy roll, down maze-like hallways, they came to a room with two police officers keeping guard. Lily asked to see Devereux and one of the men told her to wait a moment while he checked inside. He came back out with a tall man in a suit and tie.

"Lily, it is so good to see you," Kinneman said, his signature cigarette dangling from his lips. "You've helped us solve quite a case. When you've recovered we're gonna need your recount of events for our records, but it looks like this is gonna get wrapped up nicely. You helped us nab one very dangerous man. Thank you. I'm sure you'll want to see him now." He smiled. "Take care, Ms. Santos. I'll be seeing you around."

"Thank you, detective."

A nurse wheeled her inside. When she entered the room, he was already looking at her. He looked fragile as he sat upright in the flowery hospital gown. He smiled and waved her over. The nurse wheeled her up to the bed and left.

"What took you so long?" Devereux asked. "I've been waiting for you to wake up."

Lily pushed herself up slowly. She leaned in and hugged him. He hugged back tighter. Since coming to Los Angeles, the only friend she'd had was her mother. Audric Devereux, through unfortunate circumstance, had become someone she respected dearly.

"You like the cross? I had them put it on you while you were asleep. I figured it'd keep your mother close by your side."

"I thought you were dead, Audric."

"He shot me in the chest," he untied the gown from the back and lifted it off. He pointed to the scar on his sternum. "Missed my heart. It's going to put more strain on me. And this will take some time to heal," he said lifting his right hand, now in bandaging. "My surgeon says I should retire, that my heart can't take any more abuse. I say I'd go crazy just sitting around looking at pictures of missing kids. No point in staying home all day, waiting until the day I die."

"Missing kids?" Lily asked.

"Long story. Maybe I'll tell you about it sometime."

A Holoscreen played in the corner of the room. The news was on. A panel of journalists were discussing the merits and disadvantages of technological alteration to the human body. The hot-button topic in relation to the Marionette Murders, as they were apparently being called.

Lily turned to Devereux.

"It's gone public," he said. "Media can't stop talking about it. But it's all over now. We've got some tidying up to do, but it's all behind us. We've identified all the girls and located their relatives. He kidnapped seven women. Five girls dead, two of which became successful operations, not including you."

"Who were they?" Lily asked. "What were their names?"

"Andrea Cavalier, twenty-two, model. Erika Sterling, nineteen, student. Monica Yoshida, thirty-one, actress. Those were the ones that didn't even have a chance. They died from complications during the onset of neural surgery. Valerie Conlin, the first successful subject. She killed Cromwell and Levine. She died later that night from neural complications. The second one was you. And the third was Susan Devry, our last encounter at the garage." He paused and took a breath. "I failed her."

A subtle crack in his voice. She'd never seen him like this. Lily placed her hand on his forehead. She knew what was going through his mind.

"You didn't fail. I know it wasn't an easy choice, but you saved my life. I will honor Susan's life by trying to live mine."

"Yeah," was all he managed to say. The depression was sinking him. It had probably been torturing him the past two weeks, Lily thought.

"And we stopped Daneker before he had his way with that other woman in the back of the van. You saved two lives, Audric. Tell me her name. Do you know her name?"

Devereux looked at Lily. His eyes were looking for reassurance, anything to salvage the ugliness he'd plunged into. "Her name was Micah Johnson, twenty-four, student."

"Micah. I know she'll be grateful. You have no idea how you just changed her life. The important thing is this is over. The families can have closure now."

He nodded. "Yeah. Closure."

A thought hit Lily. She frowned as the idea played in her head. "Something is bothering me."

"What is it?" he said turning off the Holoscreen.

"When I was in the van with Daneker, I noticed he was stronger than a normal man. I think he had augmentations."

"I know. Kinneman filled me in. We think he might have done those to himself, although his motives are still unclear. When the Coroner's Office performed the autopsy, they also found he had an embedded receiver that allowed him to neutrally link up with and control his test subjects. We also found religious literature in his home, but as to why he went ballistic, we don't know yet."

"Audric, he had the blue lights in his eyes."

"Yeah? And?"

"Think about it. That means he was under control, too. Right?"

Devereux looked at her. He nodded his head and pursed his lips.

"There's more to this, isn't there?"

"Looks like it," Devereux said biting his lip now. "Sometimes it never ends."

She reached her hand out. He smiled and took it. They held hands taking comfort in each other's friendship. Lily thought about the road of life, weathered by unforeseen storms, and was glad to have Audric beside her.

Devereux and Lily looked out the window. Nighttime was settling in now, and the lights of Los Angeles gleamed like a big neon switchboard. Tomorrow might bring a bad day, one could never know. But tonight, they decided, the lights looked beautiful.

***

EPILOGUE

THE MAN IN THE black suit smiled. Heinrich felt it to be rehearsed time and time again, like a blade sharpened by a master craftsman.

"You are a sick man, Heinrich, but it got our attention. What better way to market your product than to have it out in public for all to see?"

"Of course, of course," Heinrich smiled back. Countless deals were brokered off smiles alone. Sometimes it wasn't just the product that sealed the deal; sometimes they were buying you. The person was the product.

"And all it cost you was— what? A couple of overpaid dicks and a few sluts?"

Heinrich opened a bottle of champagne. He poured gently into two glasses. "They lacked vision anyway."

"We want in. We like what we saw on the news. The Pentagon already has a unit it wants to test on. One of our best covert teams. Of course, we'll tell them to sign the waivers and that they'd be helping their country get a leg up, but when it's all ready to go and we've worked out the kinks, we can proceed on enemy combatants."

"So it's a deal?"

The man in the black suit got up from his chair and took a glass of champagne. "It's a deal." His lips were stiff as he swallowed the alcohol. Heinrich saw the subtle incisions on his face where he had received plastic surgery. A fairly decent job, too. He made note to ask for the name of his surgeon. A new friendship began to form and friends didn't keep secrets from each other. In fact, secrets were the common currency amongst friends like them.

"They both looked out the window.

"Great view," said the man in the black suit.

"The best."

And the plastic men in the chrome tower with their razor smiles admired the view of lights. The sun finally sank behind the horizon, and the city knew darkness again.

***

ABOUT THE AUTHOR

PEDRO INIGUEZ IS A Horror and Science-Fiction writer from Los Angeles, California. He has a love of comic books, film, literature, science, and history. When he's not reading, or writing, he enjoys painting, discussing politics, or catching up on a good movie. His short stories and poetry have appeared in various magazines and anthologies such as *Space and Time Magazine, Crossed Genres, Outposts from Beyond, Sanitarium Magazine,* and *Deserts of Fire* from Night Shade Books.

AFTERWORD

I WOULD LIKE TO personally thank you for buying and reading this book. Writing this novel has been and continues to be fulfilling for me and I hope that it is enjoyable for you to read.

Please consider taking a little extra time to help others find this book by leaving feedback where you purchased it. Your opinion about this book truly matters, both to me and to other readers.

If you have any questions, comments, suggestions or just want to say hi, please visit our publisher's web page on Indie Authors Press www.salgado-reyes.com and follow our publishers twitter: @Indie__Authors

~**Pedro Iniguez**~

Made in the USA
San Bernardino, CA
30 November 2016